BATTLE OF BRITAIN

HARRY WOODS, ENGLAND 1939–1941

by Chris Priestley

■ SCHOLASTIC

For my sister, Bonny

While the events described and some of the characters in this book may be based on actual historical events and real people, Harry Woods is a fictional character, created by the author, and his story is a work of fiction.

Scholastic Children's Books
Euston House, 24 Eversholt Street,
London, NW1 1DB, UK
A division of Scholastic Ltd
London ~ New York ~ Toronto ~ Sydney ~ Auckland
Mexico City ~ New Delhi ~ Hong Kong

Published in the UK by Scholastic Ltd, 2002

Copyright © Chris Priestley, 2002

10 digit ISBN 0 439 99423 3
13 digit ISBN 978 0439 99423 1

All rights reserved
Typeset by TW Typesetting, Midsomer Norton, Somerset
Printed in the UK by CPI Bookmarque, Croydon, CR0 4TD
Cover image reproduced by permission of the Trustees of the Imperial War Museum, London

16 18 20 19 17 15

England, 1941

Sometimes I can't remember a time when I didn't have the roar of engines or the rattle of machine-guns ringing in my ears. Sometimes it feels as though I've been a fighter pilot all my life – that I had no life before the RAF, before the War, before the Battle of Britain. But I did. Of course I did. Once I was just Harry Woods, a kid like any other kid. And I suppose that's when my story really begins…

1939

I wish I could say I joined the Volunteer Reserve of the RAF because I wanted to serve my country and all that rot, but really, when it comes right down to it, I just wanted to fly. I'd wanted to fly for as long as I could remember.

When I was a kid I used to watch swifts screeching round our house, or see swallows swooping over the summer cornfields and I'd dream of flying too. And then one day, I was up on Hunter's Hill, when a strange noise filled the air.

I looked and an aeroplane appeared over the copse – some sort of biplane, I've no idea what kind. It flew so low, its wheels almost brushed the tops of the beech trees and a dozen crows exploded from the branches in panic.

I chased after it, like a dog after a stick, running through the waist-high grass of the meadow cheering and whooping. The pilot pulled her round to the east and as he flew away he waved down at me and I waved back. *That* was the moment I decided that I had to be a pilot.

I watched him go, the sound of the engine dying away as he headed toward the horizon. I waved and waved, until my arm ached. Then I had the strangest feeling that there was someone behind me and I turned round. The field was empty. A breeze shook the long grass and waves spread out over the meadow like ripples in water. When I turned back, the plane was gone.

The RAF Volunteer Reserve gave me the opportunity to fly and I took it. I joined in January 1939. I was eighteen years old. We were all given the rank of sergeant and the RAF paid the fees for our flying lessons as long as we took the evening classes in navigation and signals and so on.

As well as the RAFVR, there was another organisation of part-time pilots: the Auxiliary Air Force. These were spare-time squadrons, a bit like the Territorial Army, except they had a reputation for being filled with toffs who lined their jackets with red silk. They were all officers of course. The VR didn't have much time for the AAF. The regular RAF didn't have much time for either of us.

I learned to fly at weekends in Tiger Moth biplanes, taught by ex-RAF bods who all seemed like something out of *Biggles*. It was fantastic, taking to the air in an open cockpit under clear blue skies. It was a wonderful summer, that summer of '39, the summer before the War.

Mum and Dad never really understood the flying thing, though. My dad's a doctor and I know he wanted me to follow him into medicine. Even so, they both seemed pleased when I told them I'd like to be an architect. Flying was just a hobby to me really.

"They're not teaching you for fun," my dad would say, and he was right of course. The whole idea of the VR and the AAF was to build up a supply of trained pilots. We all kind of knew there would be a war, and I suppose I wanted to see some action – and not be stuck in some godforsaken trench like they were in the last one.

I was in London when war was declared. It was a Sunday morning. I was visiting my sister Edith, who was training to be a nurse. We heard the PM's speech together. Chamberlain sounded tired and sad. The wireless crackled and hissed. It was 3 September 1939.

"This morning," he said. *"The British Ambassador in Berlin handed the German Government a final note stating that unless we heard from them by eleven o'clock that they were prepared at once to withdraw their troops from Poland, a state of war would exist between us."* Edith reached out and grabbed my hand. *"I have to tell you now that no such undertaking has been received, and that consequently ... this country is at war with Germany."*

Almost immediately, air-raid sirens went off and barrage balloons took to the sky, looking like great fat silver fish. We all grabbed our gas masks and waited for the bombers to fill the sky ... but none came. Not then, anyway. In fact nothing happened for so long that people called it the "Phoney War". Even so, buildings were sandbagged just in case, and a blackout was brought in, so bombers wouldn't have an easy target at night. Street lights were switched off and car headlights covered.

I was nearly killed by a tram when I was up in London. I only just jumped out of the way in time. Edith said that a doctor told her that road deaths had doubled since the blackout.

She also told me about all the accidents they had to deal with: people falling down flights of steps in the dark and walking into trees and lampposts – and each other. Eventually the powers that be painted white stripes on everything to make it a bit easier to see them.

⊥⋏⊥

I was called up to active service as soon as war broke out and spent the bitterly cold winter being knocked into shape by the RAF. We went to horribly dull lectures and learnt how to march and salute and all that rot. We learned to navigate. We learned to shoot. And of course we flew.

I flew Harts, Magisters, Harvards and Ansons, learning to fly in formation, learning how to do rolls and loops and spins, learning the stuff I would need in the months to come. At every stage we were tested and I was pleased to see I was pretty good. "Above Average" it said in my Log Book.

Some of the chaps were trained to fly bombers, of course, but me, I was going to be a fighter pilot. I suppose I should have been scared – a couple of chaps were killed just training – but I wasn't. I was just incredibly excited. *I just wanted to fly.*

In the spring they let me loose in a Hurricane, which was a whole different kettle of fish, faster than anything I'd ever flown before. It was fantastic! But it was nothing compared to the aircraft I was going to spend the war flying. It was nothing compared to the Spitfire.

I arrived home on leave on Wednesday 15 May. When my mum opened the door and saw me in my uniform she burst into tears.

"Pilot Officer Harry Woods reporting for duty," I said. She hugged me so tightly I thought my lungs would collapse. I don't know whether she was proud or sad. A bit of both maybe. Mothers are a funny lot.

My dad was in the lounge listening to the wireless. He switched it off as I walked in, stood up and shook me firmly by the hand.

"So those are the wings you've worked so hard to get?" he said, looking at the badge on my tunic.

"Yes," I said with a grin. "Sewed them on myself."

"I'll go and make us all a nice cup of tea," said Mum.

Dad and I sat down, neither of us quite knowing what to say. The clock on the mantelpiece ticked away. Dad leaned forward, looking serious.

"You know the Germans broke through the French Line this morning?"

"Yes – heard about it at the station. Looks like this is it."

Dad nodded. "I suppose it is, son." The kettle began to whistle in the kitchen.

"What do you make of Churchill, Dad?" I said. Churchill had taken over as PM a few days before.

"Well he's got to be better than Chamberlain," he said. "You need an old bulldog like Churchill if there's going to be a scrap. And there is."

"Oh please don't let's talk about the War, dear," called Mum from the kitchen.

"You remember Bob Jenkins?" said Dad.

"Bob Jenkins. Of course I know Bob. I played cricket with him."

"Well he's with the British Expeditionary Force," said Dad.

"He's only nineteen," said Mum as she came in with the tea.

"So am I," I replied rather foolishly. Mum put the tea tray down, burst into tears and ran upstairs.

"I'm sorry … I just…" I babbled.

"Come and see what's going on in the garden," said Dad. I followed him out and through the side gate, round to the back of the house.

"What on earth?" I couldn't believe my eyes. Mum's beautiful flower borders were all dug up and the place

11

looked like a building site. There were sheets of corrugated iron lying around and Dad seemed to be digging the whole place over.

The garden had always been so perfect. Mum spent every spare minute out there. It was her pride and joy. I suddenly remembered how, as a little boy, I used to follow her about with a toy wheelbarrow as she deadheaded the roses, until it was full of faded petals.

"What's all this, Dad?" I said.

"Well, the corrugated iron over there's an Anderson shelter I've bought. We're not likely to be bombed, I know, but you can't be too careful, can you? And we're going to grow our own vegetables. Do our bit. Chickens too, actually."

"Good for you, Dad. But doesn't Mum mind? About the flowers, I mean? About the roses?"

"Her idea, son."

"Well good for her, too, then," I said. "It shouldn't be for too long, anyway, should it?

"Let's hope not," he said.

Dad lit his pipe and a robin hopped down from his perch on a spade handle to tug a worm from the earth. Dad looked up at the sky. I followed his gaze, but there was nothing there. Somewhere in the distance a cuckoo sounded off.

"We don't want a hero for a son, Harry," he said without turning round. "Your mother and I are quite happy with the one we've got."

"Message received, Dad. I'll be careful."

"Good lad. Now, how about that cup of tea?"

By the time we'd walked back into the house, Mum was in the lounge smiling as if nothing had happened, handing round the biscuits and asking what I thought about the garden. I heard all the latest gossip about the village – mostly about people I could hardly remember, and then Dad took pity on me and changed the subject.

"So, tell us about the Spitfire, son," said Dad. "Is it as good as they say?"

"Better," I said. "For a start it's the most beautiful plane in the world."

"Does that matter?" said Mum with a smile.

"Well I think in a way it does," I said. "It looks good because it's so well designed. It has these beautiful thin wings. Elliptical. It's a work of art really. Pilots have a saying, actually: 'If it looks right, it *is* right.'"

"And it's fast?" said Dad.

"I'll say. There's over a thousand horsepower of Rolls Royce engine inside – the Merlin III. It'll go over 360 miles per hour."

"But how can you bear to go so fast?" said Mum. My dad just shook his head in disbelief.

"It's fantastic! Taking off, climbing at 2,500 feet a minute, up, up, up to 20,000 feet. It gets jolly cold up there too, so you're glad of the fleecy boots and the gloves – and the oxygen of course. Oh, but when you're up there above the clouds, above the world, soaring like an eagle…"

I stopped because I saw them both looking at me, and I laughed self-consciously.

"You really do love it, don't you dear? Flying, I mean," said Mum with a smile.

"Yes," I said. "Yes, I do."

"But it's not just about flying, is it son?" said Dad. "You've got those Messer… Mesher…"

"Messerschmitts. Yes, that's true. It's the Me109s we really have to look out for, they're the really fast ones. They're the best fighters the Luftwaffe – the German Air Force – have got. But there's also a 110. They have a gunner in the cockpit as well as the pilot. So do all the bombers, actually. The Junkers 87 – you know, the Stuka…"

"Yes," said Dad. "I remember those from newsreels from Poland. Hateful things. They actually have sirens on them don't they?"

14

"Yes," I said. "Frightens the living daylights out of people when they swoop down, I shouldn't wonder." Dad shook his head.

"Then there's a Junkers 88. They have four chaps in them. There's the Dornier – they call that one the 'Flying Pencil' because it's skinny and looks a bit like … well, like a flying pencil, I suppose. They have four chaps too. Oh, and Heinkels. Heinkel 111s. They have four or five chaps and guns sticking out all over the shop." I was off. "Of course we all want to prove ourselves against the Me109 pilots. Show them who's boss, that kind of thing."

"And these Me109s, as you call them – they have guns too?"

" 'Fraid so. Cannons and machine guns." Mum looked down at the table and put her hands in front of her face. "Of course, I've got some fire-power of my own. I've got eight .303 Browning machine-guns on my wings."

"Eight?" said Dad.

"Yes. Four on each wing. Three hundred rounds a piece…"

"Oh *please* can't we talk about something else?" shouted Mum. Dad stopped right there and turned to look at her. "Sorry," she said, smiling again. "All this talk about aircraft is very dull. You know I don't understand about machines."

"Sorry, Mum," I said. I held out my hand and she grabbed it tightly.

＊＊＊

I arrived at base on 24 May, eager to do my bit. The place was pretty swish as they'd been doing a lot of work on it over the winter, getting it into shape for whatever was coming up.

My squadron was in 11 Group of Fighter Command, the group covering southeast England and the group closest to the German bases in France. We were going to be in the front line.

I stood and looked out across the runway, with the dispersal huts dotted around it, hangars full of Hurricanes and Spitfires. I felt myself getting a few inches taller just standing there taking it all in.

Hurricanes had already been sent to France and Norway, so I assumed it wouldn't be long before we'd be seeing some action as well. I was pretty keen, looking back. Horribly keen.

"At least the Phoney War is over," I said to a chap in the mess. He was sitting opposite me reading a newspaper. He didn't reply.

"I said, at least the Phoney War is over. Now we can get on with it." He peeped over the top of his paper and gave me a withering look.

"It can't have seemed like much of a Phoney War to the Poles," he said.

"No … I mean … that's not what I meant…" I said.

"Or to the Czechs, or the Danes or the Norwegians," he continued. I didn't reply this time.

"And I dare say that if you were a Jew fleeing for your life from the Nazis it must have seemed pretty darned real…"

"Look," I said. "I was only trying to be sociable." He disappeared back behind his paper.

"Don't mind him," said another of the chaps. "Lenny's always like that when he's reading the paper. Come on Lenny, be nice to the man, he's new to this madhouse."

Lenny lowered his paper and thrust out his hand.

"Pilot Officer Mike Leonard," he said.

"Pilot Officer Harry Woods." I said.

I was just about to say something else, when there was a low drone outside and he stood up. All round the mess, the chaps stopped what they were doing and walked outside. I followed them.

Aircraft were descending out of a pale grey sky. A Hurricane squadron coming back from France – or rather what was left of the squadron. As they landed and came to a halt, aircrew ran and helped the pilots out, calling for help for those who were injured.

One of the pilots walked towards me, hollow-eyed, and I held out my hand and said, "Well done. Come on, I'll buy you a drink?" I must have looked such a kid, all neat and clean and grinning like an idiot.

He pushed straight past me as if he hadn't seen me, nearly knocking me off my feet. We watched him walk silently to the quarters he'd vacated weeks before. We followed him in and found him slumped on the bed fully dressed. He slept for two days straight.

⋏⋏⋏

The British Expeditionary Force was in trouble, as we found out in our briefing from our CO on the 30th. He stood in front of a large map showing the southeast of England, the Channel and the coast of France.

"As you know," he said, "the Belgian army surrendered at midnight on the 27th. The boys of the BEF have been ordered to make for the coast..." He pointed to the map. "Here – at the port of Dunkirk.

An operation code-named Operation Dynamo has been instigated to get as many of them as possible away by sea. The Germans will of course do everything in their power to stop it – and that's where we come in. The RAF have been ordered to supply air cover for the evacuation." An excited murmur went round the room.

"Now I know you Spitfire pilots have been chomping at the bit, eager to get involved – but frankly, the top brass feel that Spitfires are too darned valuable to lose by sending them to France." There were a few snorts from Hurricane pilots in the room. "In any event, that's all about to change. If we are going to get the better of the Luftwaffe, we shall have to use everything we've got. Thousands of Allied troops are staggering on to that 12-mile stretch of beach, exhausted, with the Germans snapping at their heels. The harbour has been bombed out of action and the beach shelves away so that big ships can't get close to the shore. It's going to be hard work getting them off, and they're going to need our help in trying to keep the Jerry bombers off their backs. Your squadron leaders will give you more details. Good luck, gentlemen."

It was the 31st. I'd flown many times before, but suddenly it dawned on me that this was it. The practice was over. This was the real thing. My guts suddenly felt cold and heavy, like I'd swallowed a rock. I felt dizzy, doubled up and vomited.

"No time for that, old chap," said a passing pilot cheerily, and I pulled myself together and made for my aircraft. I cringed with embarrassment but the sick feeling wore off as I walked towards my Spitfire. Then I noticed something odd: each of the other pilots in turn patted Lenny on the shoulder as they were passing. It was done almost absent-mindedly and there was no kind of reaction from Lenny at all. He just carried on getting his stuff together and climbing up into his aircraft.

As for me, I stepped up on to the wing, patted my Spit on the flank like I used to do with Blackie, our old horse, and I whispered to it. I can't tell you what I whispered, it was just stuff. It probably sounds like I'm crazy, I know, but it was just something I did. Everybody did something.

I put on my flying helmet and plugged in the R/T – the radio telephone – and my oxygen. I glanced nervously around me and checked my instrument panel over and over again. I signalled to the airman below and he yanked the chocks away from my wheels.

We taxied off in formation and then gathered speed.

As we moved off across the grass in the early morning light, the clumsy bumping finally gave way to that great feeling of floating: dull old earth giving way to air and soaring flight. It got me every time, every single time.

Off over the rooftops and steeples, the orchards, the hedgerows in blossom, the hop fields; over the cliffs and the closed-off beaches, out across the sea to the War beyond the slate-grey waters of the Channel.

We flew in tight formation and I tried to concentrate on maintaining my position as we approached the soot-black skies of Dunkirk. A huge wall of black smoke rose in front of us, a filthy cloak that turned day into night. Then a shaft of sunlight cut a slit through the clouds, hitting the sea like a searchlight. In the sea there were boats and big ships and wrecks sticking out of the waves like jawbones. Near the beach the water was flecked with the floating wreckage of ships and men, the beach studded with those who were waiting for escape. It was a Bible scene, if ever I saw one. Like the Israelites at the Red Sea with Pharaoh at their back, waiting for some kind of deliverance.

We patrolled the coast, but though we saw plenty of

action going on on the ground, we saw no sign whatsoever of the Luftwaffe, though we could see evidence of their handiwork all around. We were at the limits of our range here and we got the order to return to base before we ran out of fuel.

I have to say I felt relieved. Good, I thought, it's over and not a scratch. I banged the inside of the cockpit and grinned. I'd heard of chaps in France who only went up the one time and got blasted; bang, end of story. Not me, though.

Then a Messerschmitt shot straight past in front of me, blasting away at the Spit to my starboard. Then there was another, and another. I looked wildly around me. The radio was full of shouting and swearing. "Behind you!" someone shouted. Behind who? Behind who?

Me109s were coming down on us from all over the place, dropping out of the clouds above us. I found myself ducking, ridiculously, inside my cockpit, twitching nervously as if I was being buzzed by hornets.

A sixth sense told me there was one on my tail and I lurched wildly to avoid it, almost crashing into another Spit as I did so. I decided to loop back and try and get some kind of view of what the heck was going on.

The sea and sky spun round together like a kaleidoscope until I righted myself. I tried to get my bearings, but I couldn't see a thing. I heard someone screaming. Screaming and screaming in my headphones.

I looked about, craning my neck. Nothing. Then I saw it: an Me109 coming straight at me from above. I rolled away as it blasted at me. A Spit shot by, coughing smoke, with flames in the cockpit. A German aircraft following behind, blasting like fury. I fired at him but missed by miles. Debris was flying past, clipping my wing.

They were all around me but never in my gun sight. I could feel myself almost crying with the frustration of it. It just felt like sooner or later I was going to get hit and go down. They were better than me. It was as simple as that. The Spitfire might have been the better plane, but not with me in the cockpit.

I swung round and suddenly a Messerschmitt shot across in front of me. I fired off a quick squirt and caught the tail fin. Then there was nothing to fire at. As fast as the Germans had come they were gone, and we were left to limp back to base.

When my plane came to a halt, I found that I couldn't move. I just sat there holding the stick. Then someone slid back the cockpit canopy.

"Are you hit?" he said, but I just sat there staring out through the gun sight.

"*Are you hit?*" he shouted.

"No," I said, suddenly coming to. "No, I'm fine. I'm OK."

I hurriedly clambered out of the cockpit and jumped down, eager to be back on the ground. My legs felt as though they belonged to someone else and I thought for one terrible moment that I was going to keel over. But I didn't.

"Hit anything?" said one of the chaps.

"Well, actually, I did get a crack at an Me109."

"You did? Fantastic!"

"Yes, just clipped its tail. No idea what happened after that. Fuel was getting so low, I had to get back."

"Good show!" he said. "I didn't hit a thing – not a sausage!" I grinned. "Good for you!" he said.

"Thanks. Listen," I said, "what's that business with Lenny? You know, that thing everyone does before the patrol?"

"What thing?" he laughed.

"You know. You all patted him as you passed. I saw you." He seemed a little embarrassed.

"It's for luck, old stick," he said.

"Luck?" I said. "But why Lenny?"

"Well," he said, "it all goes back to a little incident there was a week or so back. A few of the boys were up

24

getting a bit of practice in – Lenny was one of them. Anyway, something happened to his Spit. The engine cut out completely and it started to fall out of the sky. None of the controls would respond, and he had no choice but to get out.

"He slid back the hatch and climbed out, but somehow got caught up in the cockpit and he was stuck there, half in, half out. He could see the ground hurtling towards him as the Spit started to spin.

"As the plane turned over, he was thrown clear and managed to open his chute at about 1,000 feet. The Spit crashed into an empty field, Lenny hit a copse of trees at a fair old rate of knots, and that slowed him down. Then he tumbled through a thicket, through a hedge and into a pile of … well, manure, actually."

"Manure?" I asked, smiling.

"Yes – a ruddy great pile of the stuff. Broke his landing, that's for sure. And that's all that *was* broken. He didn't have a scratch on him."

"That's incredible," I said.

"And that's why, you see. A chap like that has got to have a bit of luck to spare, don't you think? We're a superstitious lot, I suppose, but ever since then it's been a habit to pat him as we leave. One of the young chaps started it and it just sort of caught on. Silly really, I suppose, but we need all the luck we can get in this game."

"And Lenny doesn't mind?"

"Well, I don't know," he said with a smile. "Never thought to ask, now you come to mention it." He walked off and I was left standing with some of the others, watching a kestrel fluttering over the edge of the airfield.

Just then I noticed a Hurricane pilot striding across the aerodrome towards us. He didn't look too happy either. It looked like someone was for it and I looked around to see who he was heading for. Then I realized it was me.

He grabbed my lapel with one hand and looked as if he was going to swipe me with the other. Lenny stepped in between us.

"I hope you're not thinking of striking a fellow officer," Lenny said. The Hurricane pilot looked at me, then looked at Lenny, then back at me. He let me go.

"Look," I said. "What am I supposed to have done?"

"You damn near shot my tail off, you silly idiot! Damned Spitfire pilots," he snorted. "You think you're God's gift, don't you?" He stormed off.

It turned out that it wasn't an Me109 I'd shot, but this chap's Hurricane. I could have killed him. I felt terrible. And despite the fact that I could not see anything remotely funny about this at all, I thought that Lenny might *never* stop laughing about it.

"Come on," he said, finally pulling himself together, "I'll buy you a drink."

We walked across to the mess, Lenny chuckling to himself most of the way. I was smiling a little myself, by now.

"I hear you're a lucky man," I said as we sat down.

"I hear you talk to your Spitfire," said Lenny. I laughed and went a little red. "Don't blush," he said. "Barnes over there carries a bit of cot blanket in his pocket from when he was a baby. And you've never seen so many lucky rabbits' feet"

"Never really understood that," I said.

"What? Rabbits' feet?" he said

"Well, if rabbits are so lucky," I said, "they wouldn't have lost their feet in the first place, would they?"

"Good point," said Lenny, laughing. "So," he said, "what were you going to do before the War came along?"

"Architecture," I said. "I was training to be an architect. How about you?"

"I was studying History, but I'm not sure what I want to do. My dad wants me to teach like him, but

I'm not cut out for that. I don't know what I'll end up doing. Journalism maybe. Or maybe I'll go into politics, who knows? It's a bit hard to see very far ahead, isn't it?" I nodded.

"Listen, thanks for taking my side back there," I said.

"It was nothing," he said. "And sorry again about before. I just hate that 'Phoney War' business. There's nothing phoney about this war. Maybe if some of the chaps here read newspapers a little more and played ping-pong a little less..."

"They're not a bad lot," I said. "I'm not a great one for newspapers and politics myself."

He smiled. "I just think you ought to know what's going on, that's all," he said. "I think you should know what you're fighting for."

"I'm fighting for my family, I suppose," I said. "I can't say I think about anything much beyond that." He nodded.

"Yes, of course," he said. "Me too. But all I'm saying is this is not just about us and our families. We're fighting for something bigger than that, aren't we?"

"We are?" I said. "And what's that? King and Country, you mean?"

"No, no," he said with a smile. "I'm talking about freedom. Does that sound corny?"

"No," I said. "Of course not." His smile disappeared and he leant forward to whisper.

"Look," he said. "They think they're right. They are so sure they're right. The Nazis I mean. They think they're right about all this master-race business and the only way to prove they're not is to beat them. Do you know what I mean? They have to be stopped." I nodded. "And we are going to stop them, aren't we?"

"Yes," I said, raising my glass. "Yes we are."

"To freedom," he said.

"To freedom."

June 1940

On 1 June, we woke before first light. The ground crew already had the engines going on our Spits. I could see the blue glow of the exhaust flames glimmering from the familiar silhouettes. I shivered and flapped my arms up and down to get my circulation going.

My cup of tea was already cold and I tossed it on to the grass. A greasy rainbow shimmered in an oily puddle at my feet. I yawned so hard I almost dislocated my jaw.

"Get a move on, Woods," said my squadron leader.

I jogged over to my aircraft and hauled myself up on to the wing. I patted her and whispered to her and climbed into the cockpit. I checked my instruments, checked my R/T and oxygen. Everything OK. I looked around. Everyone was ready. I gave a thumbs-up to the crewman, who pulled out the chocks. We were off.

I pushed the throttle right forward, I kept the stick nice and central and eased her off the ground. Throttle back and there was the double thud of the wheels pulling up and tucking themselves in. Airborne.

The scene was amazing now. The Channel was flecked with all kinds of vessels – ordinary people bravely answering the call to come to the rescue of those stranded soldiers. As well as Royal Navy ships, there were now fishing boat and tugboats, yachts, pleasure steamers and Thames barges. It was an incredible sight.

I was over the Dunkirk beaches at 5.00 a.m. We patrolled in formation, heading east along the coast towards the new day rising. A few thousand feet below us the beach looked almost purple in that strange light and a mother-of-pearl sheen polished the sea.

Men and boats still crowded the scene, shadowy figures moved about in the sand and along the shore. Vessels of all shapes and sizes sat offshore, waiting for the Stukas to arrive. There was a click on the R/T and then my squadron leader's voice:

"Bandits dead ahead." Sure enough, there were a dozen Me110s heading away from us. "Tally ho!"

Then it was every man for himself. The Germans saw us and scattered and we scattered with them. It was all nerve now, all reflexes and adrenalin. The world speeded up and you had to go with it, like some crazy merry-go-round.

I span out of formation. There were Me109s above

us but I ignored them as much as I could. I took after a 110 that had banked off to my starboard. It disappeared into a cloud, but I kept right after it. I wasn't going to be shaken off so easily. When the cloud broke again there it was.

I steered her into my gun sights and thumbed the firing button. Tracer shot out from my guns and headed off toward the German. At first nothing happened, but then smoke began to snake out from his port engine. I came in closer.

I fired off another blast and peeled away. A whole chunk of the cockpit canopy flew off and very nearly smacked straight into me. The Messerschmitt seemed to hang in the air for a second – then it exploded and broke into pieces. There was no chance for anyone to bale out. I saw it go down, down, down and smash into the sea.

"The Royal Air Force engaged the main strength of the German Air Force, and inflicted upon them losses of at least four to one," drawled Churchill on 4 June. We were listening in the mess and there were a few sceptical snorts. Four to one? It hadn't felt like four to one.

"And the Navy, using nearly 1,000 ships of all kinds, carried over 335,000 men, French and British, out of the jaws of death and shame, to their native land and to the tasks which lie immediately ahead. We must be very careful not to assign to this deliverance the attributes of a victory."

"Not much chance of that!" shouted someone.

"Wars are not won by evacuations. But there was a victory inside this deliverance, which should be noted. It was gained by the Air Force. Many of our soldiers coming back have not seen the Air Force at work; they saw only the bombers which escaped its protective attack. They underrate its achievements..." A huge cheer went up. Churchill was trying to give the RAF some credit.

Soldiers were telling their families they hadn't seen the RAF at Dunkirk, but we were there all right. And they hadn't seen our losses.

To tell the truth, Churchill laid it on a bit thick – but we didn't complain. It felt good to be getting a pat on the back. He compared us to knights – to the Knights of the Round Table, even. It was fantastic.

"Even though large tracts of Europe and many old and famous states have fallen or may fall into the grip of the Gestapo and all the odious apparatus of Nazi rule, we shall not flag or fail. We shall go on to the end, we shall fight in France, we shall fight on the seas and oceans, we shall fight

with growing confidence and growing strength in the air, we shall defend our island, whatever the cost may be, we shall fight on the beaches, we shall fight on the landing grounds, we shall fight in the fields and in the streets, we shall fight in the hills; we shall never surrender..." More cheers.

It was quite a speech all round. He could certainly talk, old Winston. One of the chaps in our squadron could do a terrific impersonation of him. Very funny. Not too respectful though, to tell the truth, so we had to make sure the CO wasn't about.

⋏⋏⋏

On Saturday the 8th I got a lift up to London with a couple of the chaps. They were off to a club, but I'd arranged to take Edith to the flicks in Leicester Square. *Confessions of a Nazi Spy* was on and we'd both heard it was good. I hadn't seen a film in ages.

I met Edith in the Strand and we walked up through Covent Garden. London was its usual lively self, despite the rationing and blackouts and all the other things that war had brought. The place was full of servicemen, soldiers, sailors – even a few RAF here and there.

Nobody really had any idea of what was going to happen next, except that whatever it was, it was unlikely to be pleasant. Everyone was out to have a good time in whatever way they could, because it might be the last good time they had.

Even so, I was a little edgy to tell the truth. Despite Churchill's speech, the RAF was coming in for a lot of stick over Dunkirk. As far as most people were concerned we had let the side down. I could see it in the faces of the people we passed as they looked at my uniform.

Edith didn't seem to notice – or if she did, she didn't say. She was a fully fledged nurse now. She looked pretty glamorous actually, hair up, tons of make-up. Mum wouldn't have approved, but I thought she looked great. I told her a little of what I'd been through since I last saw her.

"You poor thing, Harry," she said. "Is it really dreadful?"

"Yes, it is a bit. Can be, anyway," I said. "We've been fairly lucky. One squadron lost all its pilots on their very first sortie."

"Oh my God, Harry. I had no idea..."

"Why should you?" I said. "It's not going to do morale any good to hear what's really happening out there."

"What about you, Harry?" she said. "What about your morale?"

I smiled. "You get used to it somehow," I said. "But it is hard, seeing chaps you had breakfast with not turn up for lunch." She stopped and looked at me. I could hear jazz music rising up from a cellar bar.

"Are you frightened, Harry?" The question took me back a bit. It was one I'd always avoided asking myself.

"Frightened?" I said. "I suppose I am, yes. Sometimes. You'd have to be a fool not to be."

"Poor Harry," she said, and she hugged me. A couple of sailors nearby cheered drunkenly. "But it's not going to last long, is it? The War, I mean."

"Well..." I said. "The Germans have had a bit of practice at this game. They seem to have got the hang of it."

"But they shan't win. They must know that," she said.

I smiled again. "No," I said. "Of course not, sis," I said. "We'll show them a thing or two."

"One of our doctors says the Americans will come into the War soon and it'll all be over by Christmas."

"Could be," I lied.

Well, we were in the queue, laughing and joking. We were reminiscing about when I'd fallen out of the apple tree at home and been left dangling by my braces. Dad threatened to leave me there but I started crying, so Mum made him fetch a ladder and get me down.

"You were such a cry-baby," she said.

"I was not!" I protested, though it was all too true.

"And a mummy's boy," she said.

"That is such rot," I said, laughing. Just then, two soldiers walked past.

"Bloody, 'ell, Paddy," said one of them. "Look what we've got 'ere. One of those brave pilots we've 'eard so much about."

I told him I didn't want any trouble, but he grabbed me by the lapel. He was a big lad, I realized – a little too late. He pulled me close. His breath stank of booze. His voice reeked of contempt.

"I was at Dunkirk. I had to wade through dead bodies. Where were you, eh? Where were you?" I was about to answer, when he hit me – thwack – right in the jaw. It was a heck of a punch, actually. It was all I could do to stay on my feet. Before I could decide whether to risk hitting him back, Edith jumped in front of me.

"How dare you!" she yelled at him. "Call a policeman, someone."

"Come on, Paddy, let's get out of 'ere. 'E's not

worth it." And the two soldiers walked away.

"What a horrible man," said Edith, but then I heard someone further back in the queue shout "RAF cowards!" I could see by people's faces that they took the soldier's part, not mine. I was only too happy when I reached the darkness of the cinema.

There was a newsreel about the Dunkirk evacuation. The soldiers looked grim and exhausted. On the wireless it said that they came off the boats smiling, but I didn't see anybody smiling. It was a miracle they'd got so many off, but it was still an awful mess.

All the pride I'd felt at bringing down that Me110 slipped away and I felt myself sinking lower and lower into my seat. To cap it all, the film wasn't up to much anyway. And the tickets had cost five bob!

Mum told me on the telephone that she and Dad had gone round to Mr Jenkins' house to congratulate him when they heard that his son Bob had got off Dunkirk beach unscathed. But Churchill's speech hadn't hit home with Mr Jenkins either.

"Just wanted to say how glad we were that Bob's home safe and sound," Dad had said.

"Hmmph!" snorted Mr Jenkins. He didn't invite them in.

"You must be so relieved," said Mum.

"My son was stuck on that Godawful beach for days…" said old Jenkins.

"It must have been terrible," said Mum. "But at least it's over…"

"Being strafed by Jerry aircraft, he was, and he says there was no sign of the RAF." Mum and Dad looked at each other. "Says he never saw a single British aircraft the whole time he was there. Plenty of German ones, though.

"Well I'm pleased Bob is home safe," said my dad, trying to keep the peace. "We just thought we ought to pop round."

"Yes," said Mum. "We're just happy he's home safe."

"No thanks to your son," added Mr Jenkins, poking Dad in the chest.

"Now just a minute…" said my dad, taking a step up towards the door.

"Don't you 'just a minute' me," said Mr Jenkins. "My son could have died on that beach…"

"And mine could die every time he takes off!" said my dad. "The army might be back home, but the RAF are still in France."

"Not your son, though, eh?" said Mr Jenkins. "Bunch of pansies."

"I beg your pardon?" said Dad.

"The RAF. A bunch of pansies! They're no match for Fritz and everybody knows it!"

"How dare you!" said Dad. "I ought to punch you on the nose!"

Mum had had to pull him away. She said she'd never seen him like that before. She said it was like he turned into Jimmy Cagney right before her eyes. I was proud of him. I'd have paid five bob to see him take on old Jenkins, any day of the week. Bob Jenkins was a rotten cricketer anyway.

On Monday 10 June, the Italians declared war on us as well – as if we didn't have enough on our plates with the Germans. Now we had to fight on two fronts, and we'd been stretched to the limit before. Thousands of Italians living in Britain were promptly rounded up and interned, just as the Germans had been at the start of the War.

Edith told me that an Italian restaurant in London had had its windows smashed the same night. The owner changed the flags outside, swapping them for Union Jacks. She passed by when he was doing it and she saw tears running down his cheeks. Her friends said they'd never eat there again, but she said she felt sorry for him. Typical Edith.

Four days later and the Nazis rolled into Paris. There was something about the idea of them goose-stepping about in that city that made me feel angry. I had always wanted to go there and now I felt they were spoiling it, that it would never be the same again. But then I supposed nothing would.

Then the French threw the towel in. The northern half of the country – the bit nearest to us – was occupied by the Germans. Captured Luftwaffe pilots were freed and put back in the cockpit to face us across the Channel. Now we were for it.

"What General Weygand called the Battle of France is over," said Winston on the 18th. I was sitting right by the wireless with Lenny. *"I expect the Battle of Britain is about to begin…"*

"We're ready for 'em, Winston!" shouted one of the chaps at the ping-pong table.

"The whole fury and might of the enemy must very soon be turned on us. Hitler knows that he will have to break us in this island or lose the War…"

41

"Never!" shouted someone at the back.

"If we can stand up to him, all Europe may be free and move forward into broad, sunlit uplands. But if we fail, then the life of the whole world, including the United States..."

"Come on, Yanks!"

"Shut up!"

"Shut up the lot of you!" said the CO.

"Let us therefore brace ourselves to our duties, and so bear ourselves that, if the British Empire and its Commonwealth last for a thousand years, men will say: This was their finest hour."

Edith had sent me a cartoon from the *Evening Standard*. It was by someone called Low, showing a Tommy shaking his fist at a sky full of German bombers with the words *"Very well, alone."* It seemed to capture that mood, that feeling of having our backs to the wall. I thought it was first rate, but Lenny was quick to point out that we weren't *quite* alone.

"How come?" I asked.

"Well, think about it," he said. "Just in the RAF, the Australians, New Zealanders and Canadians have all joined in. Then there are the Yank and Irish volunteers.

42

And the South Africans. And what about the Czechs and the Poles…"

"OK, OK, I get the message!" I said, putting my hands over my ears.

Lenny had a point, though. 11 Group was commanded by a Kiwi, Air Vice-Marshal Keith Park, who was terrific, flitting about between bases in his Hurricane, wearing his trademark white helmet, and 10 Group – the group north of London – was commanded by a South African, Air Vice-Marshal Leigh-Mallory.

Canadian pilots had seen plenty of action in France, and now we had Czechs and Poles training to fly our aircraft. These chaps had managed to evade the Germans all across Europe. They had seen the power of the Luftwaffe at first hand and were out for revenge.

We even had some Yanks at the base. Some Americans were so fed up with the USA staying neutral, that they came and joined up anyway. We were glad to have them. Come to think of it, Churchill was half American himself!

As I reached our front door, I heard an incredible racket coming from the hall, like a suit of armour falling down a flight of stairs. When the front door opened I saw Edith standing there with an armful of saucepans.

"Edith!" I shouted. "I didn't know you were home."

"Only arrived an hour ago. Can't stop. Mum's in frantic mode."

"Hello dear!" called Mum. "Get a move on, Edith."

I squeezed against the wall as Edith and Mum edged past with what looked like every kitchen utensil in the house. They tossed them all into an old pram and went clinking and clanking down the drive towards the village.

My dad was reading the paper in the sitting room.

"Good to see you, son. You're looking well." I looked terrible. "Sit yourself down."

"What's going on?" I said.

"Aluminium Fever," said Dad.

"Aluminium Fever?" I asked, picking up a copy of

Picture Post. Dad handed me a scrap of paper torn from a newspaper. It showed a picture of a woman holding saucepans next to a picture of some Spitfires in flight. It was addressed to "The Women of Britain". It said:

GIVE US YOUR ALUMINIUM

We want it and we want it now. New and old, of every type and description, and all of it. We will turn your pots and pans into Spitfires and Hurricanes, Blenheims and Wellingtons. I ask therefore, that everyone who has pots and pans, kettles, vacuum cleaners, hat pegs, coat hangars, shoe trees, bathroom fittings and household ornaments, cigarette boxes, or any other articles made wholly or in part of aluminium, should hand them over to the local headquarters of the Women's Voluntary Services. The need is instant. The call is urgent. Our expectations are high.

The Daily Sketch had a headline saying, "*From the frying pan into the Spitfire!*"

"Clever that, don't you think?" said Dad, "From the frying pan into the Spitfire. Like out of the frying pan and into the fire…"

"Yes, I get it, Dad," I said, smiling. "They do know that this is all baloney, don't they?" I said. "None of those pans will ever be used in a Spit," I said. "They're precision machines, you know. They're not going to make them out of old saucepans. It's all propaganda."

"Keep that thought to yourself will you, son," said Dad. "Your mother is very keen on all this. She's head of the local Women's Voluntary Service you know."

"Really? Good for Mum. But it's true though," I said.

"Maybe so, maybe not. I don't know. What I do know is that it does your mother good to feel like she's doing her bit, so let her be. As far as she's concerned, she's building you a Spitfire. What harm can it do? Every little helps."

"Point taken."

"Good lad."

"Were those your fishing rods I saw being hauled off for scrap?" I said, picking up a copy of the *Radio Times*.

"Fishing rods?" said my father with a rather shell-shocked expression on his face. "My ... my fly-fishing rods?"

"Every little helps," I said smiling behind my magazine.

Over lunch I entertained the family with tales of life in the RAF – heavily censored tales, of course. I couldn't really talk very much about the fighting, because I knew Mum just didn't want to hear about it. She had seen something in the paper showing our aircraft.

Mum asked me to describe the base, because she said I was always talking about it in my letters, but she had no idea what it was like.

"Well," I said, "there's a runway, of course – a grass one – and around that there are crew rooms and dispersal huts. That's where we sleep and sit around when we're at 'readiness'."

"Readiness?" said Edith.

"Stand-by. It means we're ready to scramble." I smiled. "Take off at the double."

"I know what scramble means," she said, slapping me round the shoulder.

"Then there's the anti-aircraft guns – ack-ack we call them – to protect the base. There's a parade ground, naturally, and a church. A mess for officers like myself and one for NCOs. Let me see … barracks, armoury, parachute store. Most important, actually, is the Ops Room."

"Ops?" said Edith.

"Sorry," I said. "Operations Room. It's where all the

info comes in about enemy positions and so forth. They get all the up-to-the-minute info, and telephone through to dispersal and send us on our way." I did an impression of someone talking into the telephone. "50 bandits, angels 20." I said. Everyone looked blank. Then Edith laughed.

"What on earth are you talking about?" she said.

"So bandits are Germans?" suggested Dad.

"Enemy aircraft, yes," I said. "Could be Italians of course, now."

"Well why don't you just say Germans?" said Edith. "It isn't any quicker to say 'bandits'."

"It isn't meant to be quicker. It's kind of a code." Edith shook her head.

"And angels are RAF aircraft?" said Mum.

"No," I said. "Angels are thousands of feet. Angels 20 means 20,000 feet. Fifteen thousand would be angels 15 and so on."

"I've never heard such nonsense," said Edith and everyone laughed.

Mum and Dad had seen a newsreel clip showing Goering, the head of the Luftwaffe. He'd been a crack pilot during the Great War, but looked like he would have a bit of a problem getting into a cockpit now.

"He's so fat," said Mum. "And so ugly."

"He is a bit of a sight," I agreed. "He's stinking rich apparently, though. He's got his own personal train."

"They're all a ghastly shower, if you ask me," said Dad. "Goebbels, Himmler ... Hitler for that matter. Like something from a horror film. It beats me how anyone could ever listen to a word they say."

"I saw some of those WAFE girls at the cinema," said Mum. "They do look very smart, don't they?"

"WAAFs, Mum," I said. "They're called WAAFs. It stands for Women's Auxiliary Air Force. We've got them at our place of course. Some of them are not bad lookers, actually, but goodness knows what they are going to do if bombs start falling..."

"What on earth do you mean?" said Edith crossly.

"Well, I just mean ... you know ... girls aren't used to that kind of thing," I said, wishing I'd never started.

"And you are, I suppose?" said Edith.

"Yes ... I mean, no. Look, it's what all the chaps are saying..."

"Oh do shut up," said Edith suddenly. "You are talking the most awful rot!"

"Edith's right, dear," said Mum. "You are talking rubbish." Dad laughed.

"OK! OK!" I said, holding up my hands. "It was a casual remark for goodness' sake; no need to shoot me down in flames!"

"Don't say that!" shouted Mum. I shrugged and laughed.

"It's just an expression…"

"Don't ever use it again," she said coldly and got up from her chair. "I'm going out into the garden." Edith and Dad looked at me.

"What?" I said.

"You idiot!" snapped Edith, and she got up to follow Mum.

"It's just an expression, Dad," I said. Dad just shook his head and sighed. Then he got up and went to his armchair to read the *Radio Times*.

"It's just an expression," I said quietly to myself.

Back at base it was the same mix of boredom and frantic activity. Jerry was launching attacks on convoys and ports on the south coast. Me109s would come over first, looking for a fight, and then Junkers 87 dive-bombers – Stukas – would swoop down on the ships in the Channel.

Most of the time we would get there too late and the damage would be done, with the Germans already high-tailing it back to France. It was frustrating to say the least. We all wanted to take on the 109s, but Fighter Command wanted us to save ourselves for the fight to come.

And when we weren't in the air we were engaged in endless debate…

"All I'm saying is, Vivien Leigh's all right…" I said.

"All right?" one of the chaps said. "All right? Have you seen *Gone With the Wind*?"

"Of course I have. But Merle Oberon is on a different level altogether."

"Rubbish!" he said.

"She is just *so* much better looking," I said. "Ask anyone."

"Absolute nonsense!" he said.

"What do you say, Lenny?" I said, giving Lenny a tap with my foot.

"What? About what?" he said, looking up from his book.

"Merle Oberon."

Lenny looked thoughtfully off in to the distance. We waited expectantly. Then he looked back at me. "And Merle Oberon is…?"

"Oh come on," I said. "You must know who Merle Oberon is. She's in *Wuthering Heights*."

"Well I've read the book," said Lenny. "But I can't remember anyone called…"

"The movie, you chump," I said. "She's an *actress*!"

"Ah, I see. She played Cathy presumably," he said.

"I don't remember who she played. We're not arguing about who she played, we're arguing about who is the most…"

"Hey, shut up you lot and listen to this!" shouted a chap over by the wireless. He turned the volume up.

"Somebody's hit a German," said the voice on the wireless. *"And he's coming down with a long streak … coming down completely out of control … and now a man's baled out by parachute. It's a Junker's 87 and he's going slap into the sea. There he goes – smash!"*

It turned out that a BBC reporter, Charles Gardner, had just set up his equipment on the cliffs at Dover when by complete fluke all this action started right in front of him. Out at sea, about 40 Stukas with an escort of Me109s were laying into a convoy. Anti-aircraft guns on the coast were blasting away at them.

He described it just as if it was a football match or something. You could hear bombs; you could hear the rattle of machine-gun fire from the fighters. There was something so odd about listening to all this on the wireless. The whole mess went totally silent.

Dad told me later how he and Mum had listened to it on the wireless. My dad had reached over to switch it off, but my mum said, no, she wanted to hear. She said it made her feel closer to me. She held my dad's hand and carried on listening.

Gardner sounded a little disappointed when the bombers headed for home, but he got very excited again when the fighters reappeared. He was like a kid. He was almost giggling.

"There are three Spitfires chasing three Messerschmitts now. Oh boy! Look at them going! Oh yes. I've never seen anything so good as this. The RAF fighters have really got these boys taped."

When he finished we all cheered. We loved it, of course, but not everyone was so keen. Dad told me there were angry letters in newspapers complaining that this just wasn't the way to go on when lives were at stake. Gardner was rapped across the knuckles and told not to do it again. But I think it made the people at home feel part of it all. It did for my mum, anyway.

Then Adolf got up on his hind legs and made some crazy speech on the 19th, blaming the war on Jews and Freemasons and arms manufacturers – which was odd, because we'd all sort of thought *he* was to blame. The newsreel showed him ranting and snarling as always.

"A great Empire will be destroyed. An Empire which it was never my intention to destroy or even to harm…" We could make peace, he said, or he would destroy the British Empire.

Well old Chamberlain had shown what happened if you gave in to bullies when he made the mistake of listening to Adolf in '39. Churchill wasn't about to make that mistake again and we told him where he could stick his peace offer.

I groaned as the airman orderly patted me on the shoulder. I gingerly opened my eyes. It wasn't yet light. I groaned again. My shoulder ached. I felt like I was a hundred years old.

"Oh hell," I said. "I was hoping it had all been some terrible dream."

" 'Fraid not, Sir. War's still on. Jerry's still expecting you."

"OK," I said. "I'm – yawn – ready for action." Then I pulled the blanket back over my head for a couple more precious minutes.

I climbed reluctantly out of bed and I got dressed over my pyjamas and put my leather Irvin jacket on to fend off the cold. Then I pulled my flying boots on and tried to focus my tired eyes, squinting into the surrounding murk.

The sun was just beginning to send out a queasy glow to the east as I stepped outside to check my aircraft. The grass was covered in a heavy dew, so heavy it looked like frost. A cockerel was crowing somewhere off in the world beyond.

I said hello to the crew who were working on my Spit. I stepped up on to the wing and then into the cockpit. I checked all the instruments, making sure I had a full tank of fuel, connected the oxygen and R/T leads of my helmet and left it on the stick. OK, I was ready.

I jumped down and walked back to the hut. I warmed my hands by the stove. I looked around the hut at the pilots slumped about the place. A couple of them looked about fifteen.

Operational training had been dropped from six months to four weeks. A lot of these sprogs never got to fire their guns until they went on their first sortie. Sometimes this was the last time too. At nineteen, I felt like a veteran.

The press called us "Dowding's Chicks". The "Chick" part was because of our youth, the "Dowding" part was after our boss – Air Chief Marshal Sir Hugh Dowding, the head of Fighter Command. Dowding was a terrific fellow, actually, though he was a bit severe. They called him "Stuffy" Dowding, though not to his face, obviously.

Lenny was asleep in his favourite chair, snoring gently. I sat down, closed my eyes and instantly went back to sleep. Sleep just closed in over me, as if I was sinking into a deep black ocean. I felt as though I could have slept for a thousand years.

Off in the distance I heard a bell ringing. It sounded like the bell my teacher used to have in the playground to call us all back to the classroom. Ring, ring, ring. I saw her standing there, ringing the bell, faster and faster, more and more frantically.

Then I was running out over the wet grass, out into the cold dawn light. Chute on, harness on, gloves and helmet on. Engine roaring. Taxiing out. Taking off. I woke up somewhere over Maidstone.

This routine would happen day after day. Ten minutes later the sky would be heaving with aircraft, friends and foe, and we were all of us fighting for our lives. Ten minutes after that the fight would be won or lost. Then, back at base, we'd do a quick headcount to see who was missing.

Then I'd give my report and the crew would run all over the Spit checking for damage, refuelling her and the like. Armourers fed the guns. I'd go to the loo and wash. Then I'd sit back down in my chair, close my eyes and wait to go up again. This was how we lived then, patrol after patrol, scramble after scramble.

One day I was having a running battle with a wasp that was pestering me. Lenny was sitting next to me, reading a book (as always). I grabbed it off him and with one movement thwacked the wasp to the floor and squashed him with the heel of my flying boot.

"Do you mind?" said Lenny, grabbing his book back.

"Sorry. Wasps. Hate them."

"Can't imagine they're too keen on you either," he said looking down at the squashed wasp and snatching his book back.

"So – what's the book?" I asked.

"*Metamorphosis*."

"Come again?"

"*Metamorphosis*."

"Hmm," I said. "Any good?"

"It is rather, yes."

"What's it about?"

"Well, funnily enough, it's about a man who wakes up to find he's turned into an insect."

I raised an eyebrow. "Doesn't sound very funny," I said.

"Not your cup of tea, I shouldn't think," he said with a smile.

"Hmm… Who's it by, then, this book of yours?"

"Kafka. Franz Kafka."

"Sounds German."

"Czech, actually," he said.

"Oh," I said.

"He did write in German, though. Maybe you should turn me in."

"Very funny. You think you're so clev—"

"Squadron scramble!"

We were at 20,000 feet when we saw them. I came down out of the sun and let off a burst of fire at one of them. Smoke started out of its starboard engine. I saw the flicker of flames. The Me110 fell away, down towards the bank of clouds. But like an idiot I followed it down.

And like a complete and utter idiot I didn't break away. Suddenly there was series of bumps as the cannon on the back of the 110 hit home. I cursed myself long and loud, but had to face facts. The control column was useless. I would have to bale out.

I slid back the cockpit cover, undid my harness and pushed myself clear. The air seemed to scoop me up as the Spit fell away from me, sinking out of sight into the clouds below. I tumbled over and over, pulled the ripcord and up went my parachute.

I was swung about rather wildly for a while, but gradually things calmed down and I found myself floating down through the cloud layer, expecting any moment that a German plane would appear out of the swirling blankness like a shark in milky water.

Then the clouds began to break up and then, quite suddenly, I was looking down on the world, like a traveller looking at a map. I looked about me for Jerry aircraft but they were all heading back to France.

The patchwork of fields below me looked rather wonderful. The cloud shadow moved away to the east and I tugged at my chute to make sure I didn't drift out to sea. The fabric fluttered and flapped like a flag.

I pulled my mask off. I heard the all-clear sounding. I heard a whistle blowing. I looked up at the blue sky and whistled back. The sun was bright now and I saw a twinkling star-like glint as a windscreen of a distant vehicle caught the light. Two gulls flew by beneath my feet. A car horn tooted.

Houses loomed into view as I descended. Trees too. What had seemed like a map now seemed like a child's model – a toy tractor on a farm track, a hump-backed barn with some milk churns outside.

The field I was heading towards had a lone white horse in it. As I got closer it whinnied and shook its head and then set off around the field at a mad gallop. I saw a land girl standing by a car and I waved and shouted, "Hello!"

I landed well, sending up a fluttering skylark. It was very calm so I didn't get dragged along the ground by the chute. As I got to my feet the land girl walked up to me.

"You *are* English aren't you?" she asked nervously.

"I certainly am," I said. A huge smile lit up her freckled face. The skylark twittered above our heads. I had never felt so alive.

August 1940

I managed to persuade Lenny to get out and go to a local dance one summer night. It was great fun, actually. We were celebrities now. You couldn't open a newspaper without seeing a Spitfire pilot grinning back at you. We were a big hit with the girls and we danced ourselves dizzy.

We managed to get a lift as far as the crossroads, but forgot that they'd taken down all the signposts to foil any Jerry paratroopers. Our navigational training came to nothing and we ended up completely lost. Lenny blamed me, of course, for suggesting the dance in the first place.

"Happy now?" said Lenny.

"Look, it's not my fault, old chap," I said.

"You said you knew the way. Of course it's your fault."

"Look, if you moaned a little less and tried to help me find out where we are…"

"And how are you going to do that? It's pitch black and you haven't the faintest idea what direction we're heading in."

"Oh, will you please…"

Suddenly we heard a rumble, a drone, getting nearer and nearer. I couldn't see a thing, but I dived headlong into a ditch anyway and Lenny followed close behind. The noise got louder and louder until whatever it was suddenly stopped right next to us.

I peered out. Instead of a Panzer division of invading Germans or whatever I'd expected, there was a tractor in the field next to me. The farmer had climbed down and was just lighting his pipe. I felt a complete fool. Still, at least he hadn't seen us.

"Er… Excuse me," I said, trying not to startle him.

"You lost?" he said with a smile.

"Yes. Yes we are."

"You're a young flyer, ain't you? One of them there Dowding's Chickens."

"Chicks," I said.

"You what?" said the farmer.

"Dowding's Chicks. It's on account of how we're so young," said Lenny.

"Not on account of how you can't fly then?" he said. He grinned. "Just kidding. Come on, I'll give you a lift."

"What are you doing, driving round in the middle of the night, if you don't mind me asking?" said Lenny.

"Doing my bit, ain't I," he said. "Doing my bit for productivity and all that. We all got to do our bit, now, eh?" We nodded. "Safer too, at night."

"You must see a lot of action from these fields," I said.

"Oh yes. I had one of those Hurricanes in my top field the other day. Made a right mess of my wheat."

"Sometimes we just have to land where we can, I'm afraid, Mr..."

"Oh 'e didn't land," he said. "'E just come down, if you get my drift."

Just then there was droning noise coming from the south and heading our way. There was no mistake this time. This time it was definitely a bomber. And it wasn't one of ours. Once again, Lenny and I jumped in the ditch and put our hands over our heads.

The droning got nearer and nearer until it was right over our heads. We closed our eyes, gritted our teeth and held our breath. Then it just as quickly moved away into the distance. Very slowly we climbed out of hiding.

The tractor driver hadn't moved, and was puffing quietly on his pipe.

"One of those Jerry bombers. Junkers they call 'em, don't they?" He pronounced Junkers with a hard "j", like in junk.

"Yunkers," said Lenny. "It's pronounced Yunkers."

"Junkers," repeated the farmer in the same way as before. "Even if those so-and-sos take over, I ain't going to be speaking no German."

Then, out of the corner of my eye, I became aware of a strange fluttering. There it was again. And again. Slowly, right in front of my face a piece of paper drifted back and forth like an autumn leaf. I plucked it from the air.

"What the…" said the farmer. "Let's 'ave a look at that there." He flicked his lighter and the three of us crowded round.

On the paper was written, in large capital letters A LAST APPEAL TO REASON BY ADOLF HITLER. Underneath was a reprint of the speech he'd made back in July. The farmer chuckled.

" 'E's a rum 'n', ain't 'e though?" Then he set the leaflet on fire, dropped it on to the road and then stamped it out with his boot. "Come on, Chickens," he said. "Hop aboard."

The tractor rattled into life and off it went with us hanging on to the side. It wasn't much faster than walking but we weren't so very far away.

"I say!" I said suddenly. "How do you know we're not spies?"

"Oh," he said. "Those Jerrys is 'ard as nails. No, I knew you was English the minute I sees you jump in that ditch."

On Tuesday 13 August a fine drizzle fell from a cygnet-grey blanket of cloud. Jerry had been hitting some of the forward bases. I'd flown over one of them after a raid and they'd made quite a mess of it. Today, we'd hopefully get the jump on them.

We spent most of the day staving off boredom and thoughts of the next scramble, but at about four o'clock we were running hell-for-leather out of our dispersal hut and not long after we were up against a flock of Jerry aircraft – Stukas, Me109s, Me110s – the whole shooting match.

We climbed to 20,000 feet and watched the bombers sail by below us at about 15,000. The Squadron Leader shouted "Tally Ho!" and we arced around behind them and dropped out of the sun. They never even saw us coming.

The Me109s were higher as usual and dived across to meet us. I looped round and found myself jumping straight onto a 109's back. I gave him a quick squirt, the aircraft wobbled slightly, flipped on to its back and then burst into flames. It dropped out of the sky, spiralling crazily down, down, through the clouds and back to earth. My first 109!

I saw a Hurricane steaming towards an Me110, guns blazing. Then he just kept on going, ploughing straight into the German. Both planes exploded into each other, scattering flaming fragments across the crowded sky.

The sky was criss-crossed with vapour trails and snaking coils of black smoke. Planes flickered by like fish in a murky pond, darting this way and that. A parachute opened. A piece of wing fluttered by. Columns of smoke rose up along the horizon. I saw Stukas standing out white against it.

They were slow and I hared after them. I swept round behind one and came in from just below. I could see the big yellow bomb hanging underneath. I was so close I couldn't miss – but miss I did. Bringing down the 109 had made me cocky. I came in too fast, overshot and missed by miles. Out of ammo, I had no choice but to run for home. The Stuka carried on with its bomb.

"Just get it sorted out!" I snapped at the mechanic and stormed off. Lenny wandered up.

"Problems?" he asked.

"Just these idiots," I said. I heard the mechanic muttering to one of the other airmen and swung back round to face him. He actually looked a little frightened. Had I changed so much?

"Look, it's my life on the line up there!" I shouted, pointing up to the sky. "If you screw up, it's me that pays the price, not you. Just do your job, OK?" I saw Lenny raise an eyebrow and I turned towards him.

"Steady on, old chap. We're all on the same side, you know."

"Stay out of it, will you Lenny?" I said.

"OK, OK," he said, holding up his hands. "Don't shoot. I'm a hero too, remember?" He grinned, but I wasn't in the mood.

"Look, Lenny…" I began. BOOM! "What the…?" BOOM! The whole place shook.

"Scramble! Scramble! Protect base!"

A Junkers 88 roared past above us. We both dived as the bomb dropped. BOOM! We picked ourselves up and ran to a trench near the ack-ack guns. The crew were already getting our Spits going and we grabbed our gear and made a dash for our aircraft.

Pieces of shrapnel and stones were raining down, pinging off the aluminium of my Spit. The take-off was total chaos, with aircraft jinking this way and that, lit up by blinding flashes. BOOM! We got away, though. Up and away and at those blasted bombers.

Below us the airmen and WAAFs were making for their shelters. The Ops Room was hit. So was one of the hangars. Smoke blinded me for a second and then I was through and out into the fight.

I chased after a Junkers but lost him before I could even think about firing. A Hurricane zipped by me, white smoke pouring out of its exhaust and the pilot climbing out of the cockpit. Ack-ack fire burst all around me.

Then I spotted an Me109 in my mirror, homing in for me. I rolled away just as he opened fire and he must have missed me by inches. BOOM! Another bomb exploded well wide of the airfield, sending clods of earth into the air.

When I righted myself I saw a Hurricane blasting away at a Dornier. He roared in so close I thought he hadn't left enough time to pull out of his dive, but at the last instant he did and the Dornier wobbled and then flipped down, nose first.

But the bombers were getting through. Clouds of black smoke rose up from around the base. A Junkers suddenly appeared heading straight for me. Instinctively, I let off a burst. But I missed him by miles and then had to spin away.

Then, as always, they were gone and there was that gnawing frustration of not having done enough. When I got back to the base I found the place in chaos. A couple of the hangars were up in flames and there were pieces of aircraft scattered across the airfield. A dog went past, limping and whimpering.

I saw the mechanic I had torn a strip off, blood trickling from a head wound, trying desperately to fix a damaged Spit while fire-fighters tackled a blaze only yards away from him. A hanger roof collapsed to my left with an almighty crunch and clang.

An ambulance swung round in front of me, swerving to avoid the severed tailplane of a Hurricane. A German pilot parachuted slowly down into the midst of all this activity, but he was already dead, hanging limply from his harness. About 50 feet up, his chute caught a spark and burst into flames and he flopped to the ground.

One of our chaps was walking backwards and forwards along a stretch of about ten feet. He was wearing pyjamas with an Irvin jacket over the top and nothing on his feet. The all-clear wailed out over everything.

Civilians and Home Guard ran this way and that, carrying stretchers and buckets of water. Chaps from the Ops room, covered in dust, helped clear a bombed out trench with their bare hands. Spits and Hurricanes landed on the pot-holed strip.

A young WAAF staggered towards me supporting an airman whose face sparkled with broken glass.

"Well?" she yelled. "Are you just going to stand there, or are you going to give me a hand?"

The gratitude of every home in our island," said Winston on the 20th, his voice growling out of the mess wireless, *"in our Empire, and indeed throughout the world, except in the abodes of the guilty, goes out to the British airmen who, undaunted by odds, unwearied in their constant challenge and mortal danger, are turning the tide of the World War by their prowess and by their devotion."*

"Cheers!" shouted one of the lads, raising a glass.

"Never in the field of human conflict was so much owed by so many to so few…"

"He must have been looking at our mess bills!" shouted someone at the back.

Later that week I spent half an hour chasing a Dornier across Kent, amazed at the speed it seemed to be doing – only to find that it was not a Dornier at all, but a fleck of dirt on my screen. I was in a foul mood and almost out of fuel when I got back to base. As I walked into the mess, I saw one of the chaps look at me and then nudge another. They all turned to face me. All except Lenny, who wasn't there.

He'd been jumped by an Me109 over the Thames estuary. He'd managed to haul his Spit back to base, but with a hole the size of a cricket ball in the side of the cockpit. He was unconscious by the time they'd got to him and he had been taken to hospital. He was in a bad way – but he'd live, they said.

It was a couple of days before I could get to see him. Hospitals always give me the shivers and this one was no exception. Sunlight poured through the high windows in diagonal shafts. The glass had been criss-crossed with tape to stop it from splintering in an air raid, and the tape cast crazy shadows on the corridor walls. I could see plum-coloured hollyhocks growing between the sandbags outside.

I asked an Aussie nurse for directions and I eventually found Lenny's room. He was sitting up in bed – reading a book as usual. I knocked and walked in.

"Harry," he said, looking up. "Good of you to come."

"Nonsense," I said. "How are you, old chap?"

"I've been better, I must say. But there are chaps a lot worse off than me." We'd talked about burns before and I knew that's what he meant. We all had a dread of being burnt to death in our aircraft. And maybe even more of a dread of being burnt and surviving.

"Your folks been in?"

"Just missed them, actually. My mother's in a bit of a state. You know what mothers are like."

"I do. I certainly do. Must be tough for them, though."

"Yes it must."

"How about your dad?"

"He never wanted me to go in the RAF in the first place, so it's difficult. He doesn't say much, but I know he thinks it's all my fault."

"I'm sure he doesn't, Lenny."

"So tell me about things. Are they coping without me back at base?

"Oh, just about," I said smiling.

"I hear things have been rather lively."

"I'll say. But look, you don't want to talk about all that, surely..."

"No I do, I really do," he said. "You've got no idea

how boring it is here. Come on, what's been happening?"

So I gave him the gen on everything that had happened in the last few weeks. It was odd talking about it. I hadn't really had much of a chance to take it all in, but telling Lenny about it brought out what a wild time it had been.

"You know the RAF bombed Berlin again last night," said Lenny.

"Yes, I know. The Germans started it, though." Jerry bombers had hit the City of London on 24 August.

"Look, that had to be an accident, those bombs falling on the City," said Lenny. "If that had been the real target they'd have flattened it. And how many times do you think Hitler is going to put up with us bombing Berlin before he goes off? It's like hitting a hornet's nest with a stick."

"Maybe so," I said. "Maybe so."

Then a nurse popped her head round the door and said I ought to be leaving so Lenny could rest.

"I say," I said when she'd gone. "She's a bit of a stunner."

"Hands off," he said with a grin. "I saw her first."

"You take good care of yourself, my friend," I said, and reached out to shake his hand.

"And you," said Lenny. "Don't get stupid up there."

"I won't. You take care and I'll see you around."

And then I left, walking through those long hospital corridors, in and out of the shadows, and into the waiting sunlight. Neither of us had mentioned Lenny's missing leg.

September 1940

It felt like the world was slowing down. I could feel my pulse in my thumb on the stick as it rested next to the red firing button. Tiny wisps of cloud were scudding across the front of my cockpit.

It was magical, like a dream. I didn't feel the harness that strapped me in, or even the cockpit around me. It just felt like I was flying up there, really flying. It was as if I had melted into the Spitfire. As if I had grown wings. I no longer had to think about turning, I just turned as a bird would, swooped as a bird would swoop.

We did our usual dance, the Luftwaffe and ourselves, round and round. Then I saw the Me109 below me, standing out against the mashed-potato clouds, the crippled cross of the swastika standing on its tail. I banked to port and dived down towards it. I could hear nothing but my own breath inside my mask. I could feel my pulse on the trigger.

I willed the German into the gun sight. Just a little more. Just a little more. Don't rush it. Wait. Wait. I could see the pilot in the cage of his cockpit. But he didn't see me.

"This is for Lenny," I said, but not out loud. Only in my head. "This one is for Lenny," I said and I pressed the fire button.

人人人

I spoke to Lenny the next day and told him about the 109. I didn't say it was for him, but he somehow seemed to know. Lenny was funny like that. It was as if he knew what I was thinking.

"Don't get sloppy up there, Harry, will you," he said. "Don't start getting sloppy."

"Who me?" I said. "Not a chance."

"You OK, Harry?" he asked.

"Me?" I said. "I'm fine. Well, maybe a little tired."

"Listen," he said, picking up a newspaper. "Have you seen this speech by Hitler? I told you that the Berlin raids would get his goat. Listen to this: *'If the British Air Force drops two or three or four thousand kilograms of bombs, then we will in one night drop 150, 250, 300 or 400 thousand kilograms. When they declare that they will increase their attacks on our cities, then we will raze their cities to the ground. We will stop the handiwork of these night air pirates, so help us God! In England they're filled with curiosity and keep asking, "Why doesn't he come?" Be calm. He's coming. He's coming!' "*

"He's a friendly sort of chap, isn't he?" I said. "What a madman. And mad enough to do it, Lenny," I said.

"Yes, Harry. He is."

⅄⅄⅄

On the 7th we busied ourselves on stand-by once again. Some of the chaps dozed, some read books or magazines, some played chess, or dominoes, or cards. Everyone had different ways of staving off the boredom and the nausea.

One of the chaps was reading *Picture Post*. It had a photo of a smiling RAF pilot on it. It was the issue from 31 August and had a heading "The Men Against Goering." The pilot on the cover was already dead.

At about 4.30 we were airborne again. It was a sunny autumn day. The afternoon sun was warming up the colours in the trees. As I climbed, I saw a game of cricket being played down below me on a village green. Someone in the crowd waved.

We assumed that Jerry was heading for our bases or

maybe the aircraft factories they'd attacked a few days before. I was climbing to patrol height, the sun lighting up my rear-view mirror, when I saw them.

"What the..." I said out loud. I heard a string of stronger exclamations coming from others in the flight.

It was a vast swarm of hundreds of Heinkels, Dorniers and Me109s, a formation bigger than anything I'd ever seen – bigger than any of us had ever seen.

"London," I muttered to myself. "They're heading for London!" I thought of Edith.

I was still climbing as they dropped the bombs. I could see them tumbling towards the docks. We were too late; too late by half. We were spectators and great bursts of white light lit up the scene.

I flew straight at them and I let go with my guns. You couldn't miss really, there were just so many of them. I fired wildly into the mass. I just kept firing, like I was in some kind of trance. There was something overwhelming about the scale of it, something hypnotic.

I looked in my mirror. The Spit playing tail-end Charlie was weaving about at the back of us, checking for enemy fighters. A shadow passed across the cockpit. I looked up but there was nothing there. I looked back in my mirror. The tail-end Charlie was gone.

Me109s. They must have been up at 25,000 feet. All thoughts of attacking the bombers had to be forgotten. This was just about saving our own necks. There were just too many of them. I swung my Spit round and twisted away from them, turning and dodging for all I was worth. At least two stayed on my tail as I shot over Tower Bridge. I turned my Spit as sharply as I could and shook them off. As I turned back, going east past the dome of St Paul's, I saw it all. It was like hell. It was like looking into the mouth of hell.

Hundreds of bottle-shaped incendiary bombs were tumbling down, turning the docks into an inferno; raining down on to streets and houses. The sky was black with smoke and the horizon red with the glow of the fires. Bomb after bomb after bomb. It was unbelievable.

I saw a warehouse collapse in a ball of flame. I saw a roof explode, spraying tiles and bricks up into the air. Ack-ack positions pounded and flak crackled in the air below us. A barrage balloon blew up to my starboard, and sank away, trailing flames.

"Cowards! Dirty cowards!" I shouted, banging my fist on the side of my cockpit in sheer frustration.

We did our best, but it wasn't nearly good enough. I could see Hurricanes and Spits blasting away at the mass of German aircraft and making no impression at all. We were like sparrows pecking a huge flock of crows. I felt useless.

Another Me109 took after me, but gave up pretty soon. They'd done their job and were getting low on fuel. The Germans were heading back. I managed to let rip at a Heinkel but it carried on regardless. And now I was out of ammo. Bitterly, I returned to base.

The place was frantic; ground crew running about like crazy. I gave my report and got ready for the next battle. Meanwhile my Spit was refuelled and rearmed. There was another wave coming in, as big as the first. It was hard to believe really. I just tried to pull myself together and steel myself to do better next time. In 40 minutes I was back up.

Again, we were too late and still climbing when we met them. Even so, I shared in a Heinkel and did some damage to a Dornier. On another day I would have been proud, but that day it felt puny considering what we were up against. The second wave hit London at about 8.30pm and dropped as many bombs as the first.

And of all those hundreds of German planes, we found out later that we had managed to down just 41. *Forty-one!* And on top of that we'd lost 28 of *our* fighters. But at least we did better than the ack-ack guns. They didn't hit any Germans at all!

The papers said that hundreds of civilians and rescue workers were killed and hundreds more were badly injured. Thank God Edith wasn't one of them. She told me later what a time she'd had of it, though. People brought in with hideous injuries, terrible burns. Women. Children.

Edith had seen Churchill touring Silvertown, one of the worst affected areas. He did a little Chaplin-type thing, twirling his hat on the end of his cane. He shouted, "Are we downhearted?" and the answer from the crowd was very firmly, "No!" Morale was high. It needed to be. The very next day the bombers came back. And they came back again and again and again.

人人人

On Sunday morning, 15 September, I sat in a chair dozing after breakfast. There was a slight breeze blowing over the aerodrome and I closed my eyes. I dreamt I was back in the meadow up near Hunter's Hill, standing in the flowing yellow grass, running my hands back and forth across the grass seeds. I was nine, maybe ten.

Behind me I heard the drone of an engine and I looked round. Over the tops of the beech trees came an aircraft, swooping in low. Not a biplane this time, but a Spitfire. It swooped so low that it sent a ripple across the grass. I ran after it, shouting and whooping.

But then I heard another noise behind me. I stopped running and turned, staring into the sun. I squinted upwards and another aircraft burst from the blinding light. A Messerschmitt 109 shot across the field towards the Spit. I shouted, knowing it was futile. I yelled as the 109's canons erupted into life.

The sirens shrieked out and I was already running as I snapped awake. Then, booming out over the speakers: "Squadrons scramble, London angels 20!"

It was another bright, clear day and we chased our shadows across the grass to our planes. As usual I patted my Spitfire on its flank and whispered a few words of encouragement before I climbed into the cockpit.

Still half-asleep, I strapped myself in and got her going, swinging round into the dazzling sun and taking my place in the formation. Then we bumped over the airfield and up into the air, wood pigeons bursting from the trees. The gilt cockerel on the top of a church spire caught the late morning sun.

"Two hundred bandits crossing Dover flying north at angels 20," said the voice on the R/T, but at that moment the War seemed far, far away. I felt as though I was soaring above the whole sorry world. My love of flying seemed to flood back into me.

This time we ignored the instructions coming from the ground and headed in an arc to the west, climbing all the while. Height was the thing and we all knew it. You just didn't stand a chance if you caught them as you were still scrabbling for altitude, because you just didn't have the speed. The other thing was to hit the bombers, not the fighters.

But then there they were, like a flock of crows or a swarm of fat black flies: a big rectangular pack of Heinkels with their escorts of Me110s and 109s. Anti-aircraft batteries were booming way below and shells were bursting all around.

This time we were early. This time we climbed above them, flying in the same direction, mirroring their formation. We each looked down at our targets. I shrugged my shoulders and took a deep breath. This one had to count. *This one had to count.*

Then we dived. The 110s screamed out to intercept us but they weren't quick enough. I flew towards the flank of a Heinkel, the rear gunner blasting away wildly. I fired a quick burst. The gunner stopped firing.

A Heinkel exploded to starboard and a piece of wing spun wildly towards me, missing my cockpit by inches. I sent out a burst and a Heinkel slumped out of formation with smoke pouring out of its engines.

RAF fighters buzzed the bombers, firing into the pack. All around me I could see our fighters climbing and diving and German planes falling and burning. We were getting through. We were finally getting through.

Edith told me later how she had stood in a crowd and watched the fight, cheering as German planes fell from the skies into the Thames and into the city they had attempted to destroy. All across London people did the same.

The battered German formation retreated back to France and I flew back to base. Fighter Command had lost over 50 planes. But we'd destroyed a quarter of theirs. If they thought we were going to roll over and die, they were wrong.

⌄⌄⌄

I got a letter from Mum and Dad telling me that they'd had a bit of excitement in the village. A German pilot had parachuted in to the field at the back of the churchyard and the local Home Guard had sent for Dad as the German had been a bit knocked about.

When Dad had got there they'd put a road block up and the Home Guard had asked Dad for his ID. Dad said it was ridiculous because he'd known the men who'd asked for it all their lives. In fact he'd helped to deliver one of them as a baby!

The pilot was being held in the church hall. A couple of old-timers had their guns trained on him, the local bobby was there, and the army was on its way.

He had a shrapnel wound on his elbow from the dogfight that brought him down, and a nasty crack on his forehead courtesy of the Home Guard. I told my dad on the telephone that it was typical – I shot them down and he patched them up.

Not that that pilot would be getting back into a Messerschmitt. He would be shipped off to Canada, double-quick, and he was lucky. At least if we came down we were on home soil – that's if we didn't end up in the drink of course!

Dad had been determined to hate him, but found himself thinking of me as he tended the wounds. He said he had been expecting to find some sort of monocled character in jackboots with a sneer on his lips and a scar down his cheek. Instead there was a young chap not much older than me, trying to look brave when in fact he had no idea what was going to happen next.

"Will I be shot?" the pilot had asked my father, apparently. My father told him that of course he wouldn't be shot and cleaned him up the best he could. The pilot thanked him and Dad told him about me being a fighter pilot.

One of the Home Guard told my dad that he shouldn't be telling Germans that sort of thing, but Dad told him not to talk such nonsense. The pilot asked what I flew.

"Spitfire," said Dad.

"Ah yes," said the German. "The famous Spitfire." Dad smiled proudly. "I shot one down only yesterday," said the pilot.

My folks also told me they'd taken in an evacuee. A kid called Peter. Edith asked Mum and Dad if they'd have him as his mum worked at the hospital and was frantic with worry. He'd already been evacuated once and had such a horrible time of it, they'd brought him back.

In fact, most of the kids who'd been evacuated at the beginning of the War were back by the following Christmas. No bombs fell, so they all came home. It made it all the worse when Jerry did start bombing, of course.

⋏⋏⋏

I got a chance to drop in on my folks for a day on the 22nd and the first person I saw when I opened the door was this evacuee of theirs. He was a funny-looking tike, thin as a rake with bony legs sticking out of his shorts. He stared at me from under a flop of blond hair.

"Peter, isn't it?" I said. He didn't reply. He just stood there staring at me. Mum came out of the kitchen.

"It's all right Peter," she said. "It's only Harry. Are you going to say hello?" But instead of saying hello, he turned on his heels and ran as fast as his little legs would take him up the stairs.

"He's still very shaken by all this," said Mum.

"It's good of you to take him in, Mum."

"Nonsense," she said. "Anyway, sit yourself down and relax. It's so lovely to see you." She gave me one of her bear-hugs. I swear she could crush an ox. "Your father will be back soon," she called from the kitchen. "And you look tired!"

I was tired, too. I flopped down in the armchair and

closed my eyes. Then I realized Peter was standing in the doorway.

"You fly Spitfires, don'tcha?"

"That I do," I said. Peter walked a little closer.

"Shot down many Jerries?" he said.

"A few," I said.

"I'd like to be a Spitfire pilot, I really would."

"It's not as much fun as it probably seems," I said. "So how do you like living in the country?"

"It's great. All the fresh air an' that."

"Your parents must be glad to know you're safe, out of harm's way? With all the bombing I mean."

"Yeah," he said. "They're getting bombed every bleedin' night, they are."

"Not sure my mother would approve of the language, old chap," I said.

"She's a nice lady, your muvver," he said. "Kind an' that."

"She is. You must be missing yours," I said.

"Yeah," he said. "An' me dad, too. 'E says them Jews are in the shelters all day."

"Does he now," I said frowning.

"Yeah," he carried on. "Says they're all cowards an' all this is their fault. 'E says we shouldn't be fightin' Hitler at all, we shouldn't—" And then I just saw red.

I suddenly thought of Lenny and what had happened to him fighting for the likes of this boy. It seemed a waste and it made me mad.

"Why you little…" I grabbed him by his jumper and pinned him against the wall. He was gasping and clawing at my wrists and his feet were six inches off the ground.

"Stop it! Stop that at once!" yelled my mother coming out from the kitchen. I let go and he dropped to the floor, slumped against the wall and the skirting board. I just stood there. I looked at Mum and I looked down at Peter. They both looked terrified. Terrified of me.

My mother darted forward and pulled the boy away to the other side of the room shielding him from me like I was a rabid dog. Now she looked angry.

"What do you think you're doing?" she shouted. "He's a boy! He's just a boy!"

"You didn't hear him." I muttered. "You didn't hear what he was saying!"

"*He's just a boy!*" she yelled again.

My mother turned her back on me and comforted Peter, who stared out from behind her arm in absolute terror. I turned on my heels and left the room; left the house and the garden, walked up over the back fields to Hunter's Hill.

I sat on the fence that borders the copse. What was happening to me? I looked down at my hands. I felt ashamed of myself. The whole thing with Lenny, the constant tension, the exhaustion – it was getting to me far more than I'd realized.

I looked up. Housemartins hunted for insects around the oaks and beeches. I'd never noticed before how much like fighters they were as they wheeled about together. It looked like a dogfight up there.

Two land girls were walking across the meadow below, talking and giggling. A farmer was feeding his horse in the shade of a huge ash tree. Suddenly Dad was standing next to me.

"Look Dad, I'm sorry about Peter. I was an ass, I'm sorry. But you should have heard what he said…"

"I think I can guess," said Dad. "His father is a Fascist, a Mosley supporter. By rights he ought to be in prison. Peter is just parroting his father's prejudices."

"Even so. How can you let him get away with that?"

"Look, do you think I only treat people I like?" said Dad. "There'd be fewer people round here if that was true, I can tell you. We don't get to choose who needs our help."

"I suppose not." I said with a shrug.

"And I've got news for you, son. You're in the same boat."

"How do you mean?" I asked.

"You're fighting for everyone, not just the people you know; not just the people you like. You don't get to choose, either." He grinned at me. "It's a pain isn't it?"

"Yes it is," I said, grinning back.

"And you'll apologize to Peter, won't you?" he said.

"Yes, I suppose so," I said

"Good lad. Shall we head back?"

"I'll follow you down. I just want a few minutes." Dad nodded and walked off down the hill.

My mother was standing in the kitchen washing up some cups and saucers. She didn't look round when I came to the door.

"I'm sorry, Mum," I said.

"So am I, dear," she said. She turned to face me with a weak smile.

"Just a bit tense at the moment," I said. "Things getting me down a bit."

"Then why won't you talk to me about them?"

"You'd only worry," I said.

"I worry anyway," she said. "Talk to me."

So I filled her in about Lenny. She wanted to cry, I

could tell, but she stopped herself. When I'd finished she came over and kissed me on the cheek like she used to do when I was a little boy.

"How's Peter?" I asked.

"A little bruised. A little frightened. He'll be all right. But he's not as tough as he'd like to seem. This is hard for him."

"That doesn't give him the right to—"

"No," she said. "It doesn't. He's wrong and we tell him he's wrong. And maybe, just maybe, we can change his mind. I hope so." She paused and adjusted some flowers in a vase on the table. "Or, of course, we could just strangle him and have done with it."

I smiled. "Point taken, Mum," I said. "I'll try not to throttle him again."

"You'll do better than that, young man. You can take him to the pictures."

"But, Mum…"

"Never mind 'But, Mum'. *Pinocchio* is on at the Plaza. You know – the new Walt Disney film. Mrs Harris says it's marvellous."

"But, *Mum*…"

"Go on," she said, pushing me through the door towards the stairs. "It'll do you good. If you hurry, you'll make the next show."

I shrugged and began to climb the stairs, knowing full well that I was never going to get out of it. I stood in the doorway of the bedroom and Peter lay playing with a toy Spit and a toy Me109. He pretended that he hadn't heard me.

On the floor was a copy of *Picture Post*. The cover showed a mother hugging her young son, both looking terrified. The headline was "THE EAST END AT WAR: *Two of Hitler's enemies*."

"Peter?" I said.

"Yeah?" he said without looking up.

"Look, sport," I said. "Sorry about before, you know. Uncalled for."

Peter carried on playing with his toy planes. I almost walked away. There seemed no way he was going to go anywhere with me. But I owed it to Mum to give it a shot.

"Who's winning?" I said, watching the pretend dogfight.

"The Spit of course," he said without turning round. "Spits are the best."

"Me109s can fly higher."

"Spits can fly faster and turn quicker."

I smiled. "I say, fancy coming to the flicks with me to see *Pinocchio*?"

I'd hardly finished speaking when he was off his

bed, barging past me and bounding down the stairs.

"Come on!" he shouted. "Or we'll miss the start!"

We didn't miss the start. When we were going to our seats, a couple of people shook me by the hand and a couple more patted me on the shoulder. Everyone loved the RAF now.

There was a newsreel showing Londoners getting on with it in spite of the bombers. It was pretty corny stuff, but it went down well and there were plenty of cheers at the mention of the "boys of the RAF" and plenty of boos every time the Germans were mentioned. It was like being at a panto.

Well, I have to say Mrs Harris was right for a change. It was pretty first rate, actually. Amazing to think that it was just a lot of drawings we were looking at, although I did think it was all a bit typical that while we were being blasted to Hell and back, the Yanks were making cartoons!

There was this terrific bit where a huge whale called Monstro was chasing Pinocchio and his father. Well, when that whale was bearing down on them, Peter squeezed up against me and peeped over my coat sleeves, grabbing my arm and jumping every time the whale made a move. Mum was right – Peter wasn't half as tough as he made out.

And when Jiminy Cricket sang "When You Wish Upon A Star" I thought the whole cinema was going to burst into tears. I felt a little tearful myself. Embarrassing really. I suppose we all had a lot to wish for.

"Here," I said, the next time I visited Lenny. "I brought you some books. I got them from that old second-hand place near the station. They looked dull so I thought you'd probably like them."

"Thanks," said Lenny. "You didn't have to waste your money on me, you know."

"What else am I going to spend it on?"

"Thought by now you'd be dating one of those WAAFs you're always talking about."

"No," I said. "Not while all this is going on."

"Live for today, old chap," he said. "You don't know what's going to happen." He glanced down at his leg.

"I know," I said. "But I don't want to think about anyone when I'm up there. I don't want to be careful. Being too careful is as bad as being careless. You just have to do what feels right, regardless. Otherwise you get... Sorry, Lenny, listen to me going on..."

"Don't worry about it. Honestly. I don't want you

feeling sorry for me, Harry. I won't have it." I smiled. He smiled back, a little weakly.

"So," I said. "Are they treating you well? Any good-looking nurses?"

"Not bad," he said. "On both counts." Another weak smile. "How are things back at base? Are they managing without me?"

"Just about, just about."

"They're fixing me up with a desk job, you know."

"That's great. A brainbox like you should be running the show, not being a donkey like the rest of us."

"Thanks Harry. I'll be glad of the work. Too much time to think here, if you know what I mean." I nodded and put my hand on his shoulder. He turned away.

"Hey," I said. "We've got a film crew coming to the base – you know, one of those Ministry of Information set-ups."

"That's something I would like to see," laughed Lenny.

"Less of the giggling," I said. "Who knows. When all this is over I just may have a career as a movie star waiting for me."

Then a nurse came in with some food on a tray.

"Visiting time's over, I'm afraid." I got up.

"Sorry. I'll leave you to it, then," I said.

"What do you think, Nurse," said Lenny. "Can you

see him in the movies?" She looked me up and down as she was leaving.

"Comedies maybe," she said, and disappeared through the door.

↓↓↓

I rang Edith when I got back. She was having a pretty rough time of it, by all accounts. She sounded older.

She asked me how Lenny was – Mum and Dad had told her about him in their last letter. I said I had taken some books in for him. She asked what they were and I said the only one I could remember was *Moby Dick* because it had a picture of a whale on it. I suppose I had whales on the brain after *Pinocchio*.

"Oh no!" she said. "You idiot!"

"What do you mean?" I asked, a bit taken aback.

"*Moby Dick*, you twit! Captain Ahab! Captain Ahab!"

"Sorry, sis. What are you talking about?" She sighed a very big sigh.

"You don't have a clue, do you? Don't you ever read a book? Captain Ahab in *Moby Dick* only has one leg, you chump. The other is bitten off by a whale!"

"Oh no," I said. "What am I going to do? I... I... Oh no, Edith. What an idiot!"

But when I spoke to Lenny on the phone he could hardly stop laughing. He said it had cheered him up no end. He said only I could have done something *that* stupid.

"Glad to have been of service," I said. And he collapsed into laughter all over again.

October 1940

The film crew arrived on the 5th October. It was a
lark at first. All the attention was pretty head-swelling,
I have to admit. We were like a bunch of school kids,
clowning about. The director got rather cross actually
and the CO came and tore a strip off us.

Well, all thoughts of Hollywood soon went out of
my head. It was tedious in the extreme. The whole
process was painfully slow. If this is what movie stars
go through every day, then they can keep it, they really
can.

The chaps from the film crew briefed us about what
they were going to do and what they wanted us to do.
It was all incredibly simple, but they still felt the need
to tell us over and over again as if we were idiots or
something.

They spent an age rearranging furniture and
waiting for the light to be just right and so forth. One
chap pointed out that he usually played a few hands of
pontoon with some of the others, but the director said
that chess would give a better impression.

All this nonsense was bad enough, but the filming itself was even worse. No sooner had the director yelled "Action!" than he yelled "Cut!" One minute he didn't like the way someone was standing, the next he didn't like the chair someone was sitting in.

One of the chaps had to pretend to be asleep until he heard the siren and then jump up and dash for his Spit. The director made the poor fellow do it over and over again. First he said he didn't look asleep. He said he looked like he was pretending.

"I am pretending!" the pilot said.

Then the director said he didn't look startled enough. Then he didn't like the way he ran. Eventually the chap snapped, and when he had been asked to do it for the umpteenth time, he jumped up from his bunk and yelled, "I hope you're not going to ask me to do it again when I ditch into the Channel!"

Then it was my go. In the next scene we had to sit around playing chess and whatever and then when he gave us the shout of "Go!" we had to run like crazy for our aircraft. I was right in front, looking very thoughtful, holding a knight, just ready to move.

"Go!" he shouted, and off we went.

"No, no, no!" he shouted, and brought us all back. He had his head in his hands and was groaning.

"Some of you are grinning. This is serious. This is for morale. This is for your folks back home. Now, let's do it properly, shall we?" We all shuffled back to our positions. "And ... action!"

I picked up my knight again and tried to look even more thoughtful than before. Then the siren went off. We jumped up. I knocked the chess table over with my knee. Papers were thrown down, pipes dropped, half-finished cups of tea left on the ground.

"No, no, no!" the director shouted, apparently. He thought we were too over-the-top this time. In fact he was so busy trying to call us back that he missed filming us taking off. This was a real scramble.

When we got back, the crews met us and set to work on patching up the aircraft. I had a jagged hole in the port wing, and the airmen looked cross with me as usual, for giving them even more work to do. The film crew were still there. The director ran over to me as we walked away from the plane.

"I know this is going to seem a liberty, but we have to get back to the footage we were shooting. The light's changing all the time..."

"You're persistent, I'll say that for you," I said.

"Look, I've got my job to do, just like you. It may not be quite so glamorous..."

101

"Glamorous," I said. "Is that what it is?"

"Yes," he said, "As a matter of fact, I think it is."

"Not long ago this place was being bombed. I wonder how glamorous you'd have found that?"

"Listen, sonny," he said, walking a little closer. "I'm based in London. You may have heard on the wireless that we've had a few bombs of our own. I take it you've heard of the Blitz?"

I came very close to thumping him there and then.

"I'm sorry," I said, "but I have work to do. I have a Combat Report to file…"

"My job is important too, you know, whatever you may think," he said. "We might not get the credit, like you chaps, but we can't all be Spitfire pilots, now can we? Now, I have your CO's assurance that you will give me every assistance. And that's an order, by the way."

"OK," I said with a shrug, walking back to where the other chaps were milling about. "What do you want?"

"OK then," he said. "I need you to do the chess scene again. Where's the blond-haired chap you were playing?"

"I'm sorry, but he can't join us, I'm afraid," I said.

"Can't," said the director with a sneer. "Can't or won't?"

"Can't. He bought it half an hour ago."

"Bought it? Oh, you mean..." He looked at the other pilots who were sharing a joke as they walked to debriefing. Then he looked back at me.

"Now," I said. "If you'll excuse me. I have that Combat Report to get in."

I was chatting to one of the WAAFs from the Ops Room at the entrance to the base. I'd seen her a few times, but we'd never spoken. Her name was Harriet. "Definitely *not* Hattie," she said. I liked her. I liked her a lot. Despite the fact that she'd nearly run me over on her way in...

She had green eyes. I'd never met anyone with green eyes before. I couldn't stop looking at them. I was trying to think of some way of asking her out, but somehow I never managed to get round to the right set of words.

Just then a Hurricane flew low over the base. It banked round and came in to land, but it was wobbling around all over the place.

"He's not going to make it," I said. The Hurricane shot over us at tree height, over the perimeter fence and into the field beyond.

"Hop in," said Harriet. "Let's go and see if he's OK." I jumped in and she drove like the clappers in the direction we'd seen the Hurricane come down. She'd have made a decent pilot, I reckon. By the time we arrived at the scene, the locals were already there.

The Hurricane had taken a few branches off a willow and pancaked into a field, coming to a halt next to a hump-backed barn. The pilot seemed to be OK, but I could hear him shouting and something didn't feel quite right.

"I think it might be better if you stayed here, just for the minute," I said. I got out of the car and trotted over. A Home Guard with pebble glasses swung round and pointed his peashooter at me. He looked about a hundred years old.

"Woah, tiger," I said, putting my hands up and smiling at him. "I'm on your side!"

He scowled and looked a little disappointed not to be able to shoot me. But he turned away to point his rifle at the pilot who was climbing out of the cockpit and shouting a stream of what were obviously swear words.

When he finally became aware of the crowd around the plane, pointing rifles and pitchforks at him, he smiled. But when no smiles came back he scowled angrily and began to climb down from his plane. He tried to brush a pitchfork away as he walked forward but the farmhand holding it shoved it towards him.

"Stay right where you are, Fritz!" yelled another of the Home Guard.

"Fritz?" yelled the pilot angrily. "You call me German?"

He was going to get shot for sure, so I pushed my way to the front.

"He's not German! Can't you recognize a Hurricane when you see one?"

"How do we know it's not a trick?" shouted one of the farmhands. "You hear about stuff like that."

"He's not English!" yelled another. "How come a Jerry's flyin' a Hurricane?"

"He's Polish, you idiot! He's on our side!"

"Don't you call me an idiot!"

"Useless Poles!" said the farmhand nearest to me. "If it wasn't for them, we wouldn't be in this mess."

"How do you work that out?" I said.

"If those cowards had stood up for themselves, none of this would have started." The Polish pilot lurched forward and it took all my strength to stop him from grabbing the farmhand. "You call me coward, you English pig? I kill you with my bare hands! I kill you

105

with bare hands!" As he lurched forward, pitchforks were levelled and rifles aimed.

"OK, OK!" I yelled. "Let's all calm down, shall we?"

"He threatened to kill me," said the farmhand. "You 'eard 'im, Bill, didn't you? Little so-and-so wanted to murder me."

"No, he didn't," I said, turning to the pilot and making a "let's just humour them and get out of here" kind of face. He spat out another stream of Polish.

"What's he saying? What's he saying? Speaka the English, mate!"

"I said you are ignorant son-of-a-dwarf and I will be happy to teach you some manners."

"Oh brother," I sighed.

The farmhand grabbed a pitchfork from a man nearby and very nearly harpooned us both with it. He was coming in for another go when a gun went off and everyone turned round. It was the old Home Guard chap I'd passed on the way in.

"Let's save it for the Germans, eh boys?" he said.

Everyone held their ground for a few minutes and then they all stepped back a little. The farmhand stuck his pitchfork in the ground and stared off into the distance.

"Having fun, boys?" said Harriet, sauntering over from the car. "Anyone for a lift?"

The Polish pilot smiled. "I would be delighted," he said.

⋏⋏⋏

After he had been debriefed and he phoned his base to tell them he was safe, the Polish pilot joined me in the mess. I bought him a drink and we sat down in the corner away from the rest of the lads.

"Gorka," he said, shaking my hand. "Waldemar Gorka."

"Harry Woods," I said. I asked him how he came to be flying a Hurricane so far from home. He looked down at the table, as if he was talking to his glass. He took a deep breath.

"I join flying club at university and learn to fly," he said. "Then I join Polish Air Force. Then I think, 'This is fantastic. This is my life now!' " I nodded and smiled again, but his expression turned grim as he went on. "Then Germans come. Russians come. We do our best, but it is not good enough.

"At end of September I get out. I say goodbye to mother, to father, to my little brother. I want to stay and fight, but father say that there is no use. I would be killed for sure. He is right. I kiss them goodbye. My mother kisses me here –" he pointed to his forehead – "and says she will pray for me. She makes sign of cross and I go.

"I fly my plane to Romania. Romanians are friends but Germans already there. Gestapo already rounding up Jews. Romanians arrest us but guards let us go. I get to Italy, then France and then England. Tell them I am flyer. They train me on Hurricanes. They make me pilot. So here I am."

"And your parents? Your brother?"

"Dead. All dead," he said, taking another drink. I didn't know what to say.

"I'm sorry," I said finally. "It makes me feel even worse about what happened back there with the farm lad. What with you fighting for England after everything that's happened to you."

"I don't fight for England," he said with a wave of his hand. "I fight for *Poland*! I fight in RAF only because English give me plane, give me bullets. Bullets to kill Germans. To kill them like they kill my people." He was wild-eyed now and leaned closer to me to whisper in my face. "Know what I think when they bomb London?" I shook my head. "I think 'Good! Let them see what war is like!' " I looked away. He calmed a little. "How about you? What you fight for, English? King and Country?"

I shook my head. "Someone else asked me that a long time ago," I said smiling. "Then I said I was fighting for my family. Down here, I'd still stay the same thing … but up there, I'm not thinking of anyone but me. Up there I'm just fighting for my life, nothing more than that."

He nodded. "Look, English, I sorry if I don't talk like you gentlemen of RAF. I am Polish. Understand?" I smiled weakly and nodded my head, although I didn't really understand at all. How could I?

"Don't apologize for farmer. He think I am German. He want to kill me because I am German. If German pilot lands near me I shoot him dead, and they do the same to me. This I understand." He drained his drink and asked for another. "I hear about German pilot they shot down. He picked up by Home Guard. They take him to pub and buy him drink before taking him in! They buy him drink!"

I laughed. I hadn't the heart to tell him we'd had a German pilot in the mess only the week before when he'd baled out near the base. "We are a funny lot, I suppose," I said. But he didn't laugh.

"Look, war is not cricket match. I hear English pilot talk about dogfight being like – how do you call...?" He made a fencing motion in the air.

"Like a fencing match? Like a duel?"

"A duel, yes," he said. Then he banged his fist on the counter. "It is *not* like duel. It is like knife fight in back alley. You dodge your enemy, you avoid his attack, you see your chance, you stick him in guts and run. In. Out. Is it not true?"

"Well," I said, laughing. "I've heard it described more poetically, but you're right, people do talk a lot of rot about jousting and the like. It never feels like that to me. Mostly it's just staying alive."

"And shooting down Germans," he added.

"And shooting down Germans," I agreed, but I couldn't quite compete with his thirst for German blood.

I liked him, though. Admired him too, I suppose. He was a tough nut, that's for sure. For all my months of experience, I felt a kid again next to him.

"Look, I make you a deal," he said. "I fight for you freedom. I fight to keep England free – free for the cricket – free from German dogs. Then we free Poland. No Germans, no Russians – we kick them all out, OK? We free my country. We drink to Poland!"

"To Poland," I said. "To freedom."

"To freedom!"

∧∧∧

I arranged to meet and talk to Lenny about the desk job he'd been given. We met up in St James Park in London. He was already there when I arrived and I saw him standing, looking off towards Whitehall. He was wearing his new leg. If you didn't know, you'd never have guessed. Only I *did* know.

"I've brought some of the gang with me, if that's all right?" Lenny turned round, startled slightly from his thoughts, and then his face mellowed and finally cracked into a grin as they all walked up behind me.

"Good grief!" he said. "You're all still alive! Those Germans must be getting slow."

They all came in to ruffle his hair and punch his shoulder. One of the chaps jostled him a little too roughly, and for one awful moment it looked like he was going to fall over. Everyone went quiet as Lenny managed to stay upright.

"Not as steady on my pins as I used to be," said Lenny with a grin.

"So, Lenny," said one of the chaps. "How did you

get on with those nurses, then? We all know what nurses are like."

"Hey – watch your mouth," I said, laughing. "My sister's a nurse."

"Whoops! Sorry, Woody. Don't happen to have her number do you?" I thumped him in the shoulder.

"Ow! That hurt, you oaf! That's my bowling arm, too."

"You can't bowl to save your life," said Lenny.

"True. True. So anyway how are you, you old misery?"

"Missing you all dreadfully, of course," he said with a sarcastic raise of one eyebrow.

"Of course. Goes without saying, old chap."

And then we were off. We were more like a group of students than a group of seasoned fighters. The sun shone and golden leaves occasionally fluttered down. As I looked across at them smiling and joking, we all seemed young again.

We stayed quite a long time. I think we were all reluctant to be the first to talk about leaving. Someone produced a hip flask of whisky – something he'd bought on the black market – and tiny glasses were pulled from jacket pockets, with spares for Lenny and me. We waited for a policeman to walk past and then we poured a tot into each glass.

"Absent friends!" said somebody. We raised our glasses and clinked them together.

"Absent friends!" I drank a mouthful and spat it out. Everyone did the same. It was vile!

It really was time to move off then. Lenny shook everyone's hand and he looked almost like his old self. I told him to take care of himself and he told me to do the same. Then, as each man left, he absent-mindedly patted Lenny on the shoulder, just as they used to.

人人人

The immediate threat of invasion was gone now, but things were scarcely any easier. We had made the Germans think twice about daylight bombing raids, but that didn't stop them bombing London every night.

At the end of October, we were patrolling along the Thames estuary when I flew over London from the east. It was quite a sight. All across the city there were bombed-out buildings, roofless, with black and hollow windows and walls all scorched and pock marked. Piles of rubble filled the streets.

We were heading back when the Messerschmitts jumped us. They tore down like hawks, scattering us.

It was mayhem. The Spit to starboard crumpled in on itself and went down in flames.

They seemed to be everywhere but no matter what I did I couldn't get a clear view of them. That same feeling of frustration, of helplessness. The same feeling of wanting to puke that I'd had since my first patrol.

I told myself to be calm. "Come on, come on," I said, "get on with it. You've done this a hundred times before," as if saying it would make it all right. As if anyone could ever get *used* to this.

It was like standing on a cliff with just your heels touching, leaning out, fear holding you back, Death pulling you on – and we looked over that cliff every day. Every day. Maybe it was only luck that saved you from falling. And maybe my luck was running out.

Suddenly there was a bomber right in front of me. "Pull up! Pull up, you idiot!" I yelled, and my hands obeyed, yanking back on the stick in the nick of time. "Idiot. Idiot," I muttered to myself. "Get a grip!"

Then a dull thud and bump. I was hit. And I never even saw the plane that hit me. I just felt a jolt – and then two more – then a teeth-clenching pain seared through my right leg. I could see daylight through the floor of the cockpit. I could feel cold air rushing past me.

I decided to make a dash for base, but the plane

wouldn't respond. The R/T was dead and whistled in my ear. I was losing altitude rapidly and I now could smell burning. Glycol fumes were leaking into the cockpit.

"No, no, please, please…" Panic shot through me as I realized the fuel tank might be about to blow. "Please, please…"

Then a voice said, "Bale out!" and then again – "Bale out!" But I just sat there staring at the control panel and at the flames that had begun to appear behind it. "Bale out!" a voice screamed in my ear. *My* voice.

This time I took notice. I slid back the cockpit cover, relieved – very relieved – that it slid back so easily, and then I undid my harness and climbed out, remembering at the last second to disengage my oxygen and radio.

I was out, free of my aircraft, tumbling wildly in the air – there was the sky, there was my plane arcing away on a streamer of black smoke, there was the sky again, there was my plane crashing into the sea. I pulled the ripcord.

I was jerked back by the parachute as air punched into it, opening it up to mushroom above me. I swung there like a puppet, winded and gasping for breath. I looked down at my leg. It felt like a bear was gnawing on it but it was still in one piece. For now anyway.

Dogfights growled on above me as I drifted down. As I spun gently, dizzyingly, back and forth, I caught glimpses of the English coast, then the French, then England again. I could hear sirens wailing in the distance, the boom and thud of anti-aircraft fire. I could see the cliffs and the downland beyond. And I could see the huge empty expanse of cold grey water towards which I was heading.

Then I heard it – right behind me. A weird noise droning and roaring and screaming behind me. An Me109 diving towards me with guns blazing, twinkling like stars, clattering like hail on a tin roof.

There was nothing I could do. Nowhere I could go. Shells whistled past me on either side. A kind of weird calm came over me. I thought of Mum and Dad, and Edith, and Lenny. I thought about Waldemar and my lovely green-eyed WAAF. All in those seconds. I just thought, OK then. If this is it, OK. Maybe my turn had finally come.

But then the Messerschmitt shuddered and twitched and banked away. The pilot had no chance. I saw flames light up the cockpit like a lantern and it spun round out of control. Then there was an explosion and it broke up into a dozen pieces, falling like meteors against the cliffs.

I had hardly taken this in before I realized I had to

get my parachute off and fast. I had to release it just before I hit the sea otherwise it would drag me under. I gave the release mechanism a ninety-degree twist and then a hefty thump. Nothing happened.

And then smack – I hit the water. The calmness I'd felt in the face of being shot had left me completely now as I struggled to save myself from drowning. I wasn't going to die a sailor's death – not if I could help it. I hit and tugged and swore and finally the chute came loose and drifted away like a huge jellyfish.

All I had to do now was inflate my lifejacket and hope that someone saw me land and was coming to pick me up. The water was freezing. I could feel my legs going numb and it felt good because it meant I didn't feel the pain any more.

I looked up and the blue sky was scribbled all over with chalk-white vapour trails. In the distance I could hear the hum and buzz of engines, the rattle of gunfire. Again, it occurred to me that this was it for me, that I had swapped the sudden death the Messerschmitt offered, for the far worse fate of slowly freezing in the October sea.

Suddenly, an Me109 tore out of the east, diagonally downwards, belching black smoke. It spluttered and whined and drifted inland to crash out of sight. Then

I realized that the pilot had baled out. And he was heading my way...

The Jerry pilot landed about a hundred yards away from me and made a much better job of getting out of his parachute. He bobbed in and out of view behind the grey waves, and he seemed to be drifting towards me.

I didn't know what to do at first. I could hardly carry on ignoring him, as we were the only things out here but haddock. And anyway, maybe we were both going to die here. Maybe he was going to be the last person I saw in my life.

"Hello!" I shouted, immediately feeling a little foolish.

"Hello!" he shouted back. "Are you hurt?"

"A little, yes!" I shouted. "How about you?"

"A little, also! You are Spitfire?"

"Yes. And you? You're a 109 pilot?"

"Yes. The Spitfire is good plane?"

"It is. The 109's pretty good, though."

"Pretty good. Yes."

The cold had numbed the pain in my leg, but I knew that if we stayed here much longer, the cold would numb the rest of me too and I'd be a goner. Suddenly, being hit by the Messerschmitt's guns seemed appealingly fast and final.

"It is cold, is it not?" said the German, as if he read my thoughts.

"Yes. Very," I said.

"Are we to die then, Englishman?"

"No!" I shouted.

"Good," he shouted back. "I am not ready to die."

"Who is?" I shouted.

Then I heard the drone of an engine over my shoulder. I turned to see a fishing boat heading for us. I whooped and shouted and waved and shouted and so did the German.

"Over here! Over here!" I yelled. The boat came in close and they hauled me up and on to the deck.

"You'd better get out of those wet things or you'll catch your death," said one of the crew, tossing me a blanket. "How's that wound?" The trouser leg was chewed up and bloody.

"OK, I think," I said, struggling to get out of my flying suit. But out of the water, it started to hurt like hell again.

"Let's go get your friend, there," said the skipper. The boat pulled up alongside the German pilot.

"*Danke, danke!*" he shouted as they reached for him.

"He's German!" yelled one of them.

"I'm not having any Jerry in my boat," said the

119

skipper. "The fish can have 'im if they want 'im. Let 'im drown!"

The boat started to turn for shore, with the German flailing and yelling.

"No!" I shouted, surprising myself, and everyone else, with the violence in my voice. "Pick him up!"

They all turned to face me.

"And why the hell should I? Murdering swine that they are. A minute ago 'e was trying to kill you!"

"I know," I said. "I know that. But we can't just let him drown. We have to be different. If we're going to be as bad as the Nazis then what's the point? If we leave him there, then *what are we fighting for*? If we're just the same as them, then what are we fighting for?"

They all looked at me. A flag fluttered at the top of the mast and the boat creaked and groaned in the swell. The German's cries for help grew fainter.

"OK," said the skipper with a sigh. "Fish 'im out."

The boat turned again and they hauled the German out, though with a lot less care than they had with me. Even so, the crewman who had thrown me a blanket did the same with the German and he duly stripped and wrapped himself up, wincing at some injury to his side.

Someone appeared with a mug of tea and a shot of brandy. We both sat there in silence as the engine

120

chugged and gulls hung in the breeze around us, crying like children. My leg throbbed and I didn't dare look for fear of what I'd see.

"Blasted Nazis," said one of the crew.

"I am not a Nazi," said the pilot. "I am just a German. I love my country."

"Then why didn't you stay there, you swine?" shouted another man. The German looked away, down at the deck, but the man leaned closer and continued. "Look at all this," he said with a wild wave of his hand that took in me, the dogfight above and the whole splintered and bloody world. "Look at it! Don't tell me you love your country, or so help me I'll throw you back in!"

The skipper came over and pulled him away.

"You'll have to forgive us," he said to the German. "We haven't forgotten what it was like picking soldiers off the beach at Dunkirk, with you cowards trying to kill us all for doing it. Most likely we'll never forget it. I don't think I'll ever get the smell of that beach out of this boat."

"I am sorry," said the German.

"Shut up," said the skipper coldly, "Or I'll throw you back in myself."

They left us alone. I could think of nothing to say and so I kept quiet. The German looked away from me and out to sea.

"I flew raids at Dunkirk," he said suddenly. "We fighters gave protection to the Heinkels bombing the beaches and the waiting ships. On 1 June it was different. We flew in low, guns blasting."

It was 1 June when I had shot down the 110. It was odd to think we were all there that day – these fishermen, the German and me.

"As you came in you could see the men below, the lines of men, run for their lives, running for the cover of the dunes. I saw a man turn, and freeze, like a rabbit. As he turned I saw the light glint on his spectacles. Can you believe that? I was so low I saw that, and I saw the shells bursting in the sand in a line towards him.

"The men, they ran for the dunes. But if they stayed in the dunes they could not get off the beach and so they had to come back to their lines and queue for the boats and ships offshore. They came back and so did we. Black smoke rose up everywhere, from burning ships and bombed-out buildings.

"We would fly through these columns of smoke, down towards the men, firing our guns into them." He shook his head. "That was no job for a Luftwaffe pilot. There was no honour in that."

I looked at him but he stayed turned away. In the

end I turned away too. I felt like he wanted me to say something, to say it was OK. But I couldn't – no one could. As for honour; was there honour in any of this? And what would I have done in his place? I just didn't know any more.

A kittiwake flew alongside me, only a couple of yards away, its face level with mine. It turned and seemed to look straight at me, its head cocked to one side slightly. Its black eyes glinted and then it banked away from me and glided clear of the boat and out of sight.

I looked back towards the German. At first I thought he was just hanging his head and looking at the deck, but then I realized he was slumped forward. I got up and caught him as he fell and sat him up again. I put my arm around him.

A pool of deep red blood was sinking into the wooden decking below him and the pale grey blanket was soaked with it. His pale hands were cold. I whispered to him. I asked him his name, but there was no reply. He was dead.

He was dead and suddenly I wanted to know his name. Suddenly I had the weirdest feeling that I had more in common with this man than with anyone else I knew. His head rested against my shoulder and I put my arm around him to stop him falling.

And then, in the midst of those staring fishermen, I did something I had never done in the whole course of the war. I began to cry...

Epilogue

1941

Anyway, my leg was patched up. They pulled a few pieces of shrapnel out and stitched me up, good as new – or almost, anyway – and before I knew it I was back in the cockpit. I ended up with this rather good scar in my calf shaped like the letter "m" or the way little kids draw birds.

Then one day in April '41, I was lying on my bunk reading a book Lenny had sent me. One of the orderlies came in and gave me a package that had arrived from my folks. I used a letter from Harriet to keep my place, closed the book and opened it up.

There was a copy of a pamphlet the Government had brought out. The cover showed vapour trails against a darkening sky and the words *The Battle of Britain*. Underneath that, across the black silhouette of a building, was written: *August–October 1940*.

The Air Ministry had published it, so it was full of stuff about RAF tactics, with diagrams and the like, and maps covered in arrows. There was a photo of laughing pilots walking across a sunlit aerodrome, hair and scarves blowing in the breeze. I wondered how many of them were still alive.

The pamphlet made it all seem much less of a shambles than it felt at the time. The dawn scrambles and the rabid dogfights had all been smartened up and dusted down. There were little drawings of planes with dotted lines coming from their guns and others with smoke trailing out. It all looked so clean and simple. No blood or pain or burning. No screaming. I couldn't read it then and haven't since.

Mum and Dad wrote and said they were so proud of me. They said I was part of history now. I wrote back and told him so were they. So was Edith. So was Lenny. Harriet. We all were.

But there was truth in it. We had made a difference, we "Few" – I had to admit it. We hadn't beaten the Nazis, but we'd shown they couldn't get everything their own way. We'd given the bully a black eye and winded him a little. And maybe there was honour in that after all. Yes, I think that maybe there was.

Historical Note

Officially, the Battle of Britain was fought between 8 August and 30 October 1940 and was the first time that aircraft had played such a decisive role in the War. As well as ensuring that Britain remained free of German control, and free of Nazi deportations to concentration camps, the battle proved to be a major turning point in the War. It helped to convince the Americans to enter the War on the side of the Allies. British resistance also meant that there would be a base from which to bomb German forces (and civilians) and eventually launch an allied invasion of Europe in June 1944.

From the outset, the Germans knew that if they were to invade Britain successfully, they would have to put the RAF out of action first. The German air force (Luftwaffe) began to attack British shipping convoys in the Channel, to disrupt trade, to stop supplies reaching British shores from other countries, and to lure Spitfires and Hurricanes into dogfights over the sea.

During the Battle of Britain, RAF Fighter Command was led by Air Vice-Marshal Sir Hugh Dowding. It was divided into four Groups: 10 Group covered the West Country, 11 Group covered the South East, 12 Group covered the area roughly from London to York, and 13 Group covered the remaining North of England, Scotland and Northern Ireland.

11 Group was commanded by Air Vice-Marshal Keith Park from its HQ in Uxbridge, and was divided into sectors, each with its own Sector Station – Biggin Hill in Kent being perhaps the most famous. As it was closest to German Occupied France, 11 Group was the first line of defence during the Battle of Britain and squadrons in this Group were reinforced from squadrons in other groups to keep them up to full strength. Although Harry Woods is fictional, it is a squadron in 11 Group in which he is seen to serve.

The odds were in favour of a German victory at the beginning of the Battle of Britain. The Luftwaffe were well equipped and had well-trained, battle-hardened pilots and crews and the RAF had experienced heavy losses in France and Norway and during the Dunkirk evacuation. At the end of June it had less than 400 Spitfires and Hurricanes for the defence of the whole country. But Britain did have one secret weapon.

Radar, or Radio Direction Finding (RDF) as it was known, was first developed in 1935. It used short-wave radio pulses to pick up incoming aircraft. The radio pulses bounced back and were captured by a cathode ray tube, showing up as blips of light on a glass screen. By 1939 there were a string of radar stations along the coast from Shetland to the south coast of England.

Information gathered by radar stations (and from members of the Observer Corps dotted around the coast) was relayed by landline to the Filter Room at Fighter Command HQ at Bentley Priory in Stanmore near London. The aircraft were plotted on a large map table and then the information was relayed to the Group Headquarters and then to Sector Stations (airfields). Group commanders decided which Sector Stations to activate. Sector Station commanders decided which squadrons should fly.

Radar had its problems though. Radar picked up all sorts of things – clouds, flocks of birds etc – as well as planes. Height readings were very inaccurate and although it might only take four minutes to warn the squadrons, it only took six minutes for German planes to cross the Channel. Luckily for the RAF, Messerschmitts were at the limit of their range by the time they got to England and Me109s had hardly any fuel in their tanks for dogfights over southern England and could barely reach London.

Radar was a secret and there was a lot of speculation in the country about what the radar stations with their huge masts and antenna were for. The WAAFs, like Harriet in this story, who worked in the airfield Ops rooms, were sworn to secrecy and pilots like Harry would not need to be told. The Germans knew we had it, but failed to put it out of action during their attacks on 12 August.

Germans also failed to follow through on their attacks on RAF airfields. Too often they targeted the smaller satellite airfields rather than the important sector airfields. Even so, they did kill many pilots and ground crew and destroyed valuable aircraft. Though it was terrible for the people of London, it was a let off for the RAF when Hitler changed tactics and started bombing cities instead.

Civilian losses became heavier and heavier as the Luftwaffe's bombs rained down. Over 13,000 Londoners had been killed by the end of 1940 and another 18,000 hospitalized. Thousands more were killed in other cities across the country. Despite this, most people learned to cope with the bombing, and many were eventually able to sleep through it!

Pilot losses were horrendous during the Battle of Britain; at the end of August 1940, RAF pilot losses were approaching 120 men a week. Replacing pilots was an even bigger problem than replacing aircraft, as operational training time was shortened and shortened, with many pilots entering combat never having fired their guns before. Many only flew one fatal sortie.

More than 80% of the 3,080 aircrew listed were British, but those that were not had often volunteered, making their way to Britain at their own cost and often at great personal risk, often escaping from the advancing German army. Six of the twelve top-scoring Fighter Command pilots were from countries other than Britain.

Most Polish pilots, like the fictional Waldemar in this story, were more highly trained than their British counterparts, but as they rarely spoke fluent English, they had British squadron and flight commanders allocated to their squadrons.

Although the Polish squadrons did not become operational until August 1940, they accounted for 7.5% of all the aircraft shot down by the RAF, and the Polish 303 Squadron had the highest score rate in Fighter Command.

Nationality of aircrew involved in the Battle of Britain:

British	2,543	(418 killed)
Polish	147	(30 killed)
New Zealand	101	(14 killed)
Canadian	94	(20 killed)
Czech	87	(8 killed)
Belgian	29	(6 killed)
South African	22	(14 killed)
Free French	14	(0 killed)
Irish	10	(0 killed)
United States	7	(1 killed)
S Rhodesian	2	(0 killed)
Jamaican	1	(0 killed)
Palestinian	1	(0 killed)
Total	**3080**	**(520 killed)**

The Home Guard

There was a constant threat and fear of invasion in 1940 and the government made a radio appeal in May for any men not already conscripted (because they were too old, for instance) to form platoons of Local Defence Volunteers. Renamed the Home Guard by Churchill, one million men had joined by August – far more than expected. The government could not afford to arm them all and so they made do with whatever they could lay their hands on.

Timeline

30 July 1936 RAF Volunteer Reserve (RAFVR) is formed.

13 March 1938 Germany, led by Chancellor Adolf Hitler, annexes Austria.

June 1938 Spitfires first enter service with 19 Squadron, RAF Duxford in Cambridgeshire.

15 March 1939 Germans invade Czechoslovakia.

23 March 1939 Britain and France declare they will defend Belgium, Holland and Switzerland from German attack.

6 April 1939 Britain, France and Poland sign mutual assistance pact.

28 June 1939 Women's Auxilliary Air Force (WAAF) is formed.

1 September 1939 Germans invade Poland. RAF Reserve & RAFVR called up for active service.

2 September 1939 RAF deployed in France.

3 September 1939 Britain declares war on Germany after it refuses to withdraw troops from Poland.

27 September 1939 Warsaw surrenders.

12 October 1939 British troops sent to France as British Expeditionary Force (BEF).

1 January 1940 Two million British 19-27 year olds are conscripted into the Armed Forces.

9 April 1940 Germans launch full-scale invasion of Norway.

10 May 1940 Germans attack France, Belgium, Holland and Luxemburg. Chamberlain government falls and he is succeeded as British PM by Winston Churchill, who appoints Lord Beaverbrook as Minister of Aircraft Production.

15 May 1940 Germans break through the French line.

25 May 1940 British Foreign Secretary, Anthony Eden, authorizes the withdrawal of the BEF to Dunkirk.

31 May 1940 RAF provide air cover for the evacuation of Dunkirk.

4 June 1940 Operation Dynamo completes the evacuation of 338,000 British and allied troops from Dunkirk.

18 June 1940 Churchill famously states: *"The Battle of France is over. I expect the Battle of Britain is about to begin."*

22 June 1940 France surrenders to the Germans.

7 July 1940 Hitler issues a directive for the "War against England".

10 July 1940 Beaverbrook calls on British housewives

to donate anything aluminium for use in aircraft manufacture. British pilot operational training cut from six months to four weeks.

16 July 1940 Hitler orders "Operation Sealion", his plan for the invasion of Britain by a surprise landing of troops on the south coast.

19 July 1940 Hitler offers peace to Britain but Britain rejects his terms.

1 August 1940 Hitler orders the Luftwaffe to overpower the RAF "in the shortest possible time".

2 August 1940 Commander-in-Chief of the Luftwaffe, Hermann Goering, orders Adlertag (Day of the Eagles) – a plan to destroy British air power and open the way for invasion.

12 August 1940 German raids against radar stations on the south coast.

13 August 1940 Adlertag begins in poor weather – the German date for the start of the battle.

15 August 1940 British radar stations attacked again.

17 August 1940 British pilot operational training cut again – from four to two weeks.

18 August 1940 German attacks on RAF fighter airfields.

20 August 1940 Churchill makes his *"Never in the field of human conflict"* speech to Parliament.

24/25 August 1940 German bombs fall on Slough, Richmond Park, Dulwich and the City.

25/26 August 1940 nighttime raid on Berlin by Bomber Command in retaliation for bombing of the City.

28/29 August 1940 Germans bomb London suburbs.

29 August 1940 British air raid on Berlin.

30 August 1940 RAF bases bombed.

31 August 1940 Hitler postpones "Operation Sealion".

1 September 1940 RAF bases bombed.

5 September 1940 Hitler switches bombing campaign to towns and cities, including London.

7 September 1940 Mass daylight air raid on London. 448 civilians killed and 1,600 injured.

15 September 1940 Fighter Command destroys 25% of a German air assault on London. (Battle of Britain Day.)

17 September 1940 "Operation Sealion" postponed indefinitely.

18 September 1940 Luftwaffe forced to switch to nighttime raids because of heavy losses.

30 September 1940 Blitz begins – nightly bombing campaign against London.

14 November 1940 Coventry devastated by German bombers.

29 December 1940 Biggest air raid of War with a third of City of London destroyed.

March 1941 Air Ministry publishes a pamphlet called *Battle of Britain*. More than a million sold. The Ministry chooses 8 August as the official start of the Battle and 31 October as the end.

Pilots of a Spitfire squadron dash to their aircraft during a scramble.

Flights of Spitfires on patrol duty in July 1940.

A Messerschmitt 110 fighter-bomber shot down in July 1940.

A Heinkel 111 aircraft over the River Thames, London.

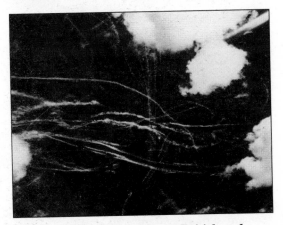

Vapour trails left in the sky by British and German aircraft after a dogfight.

These pilots are coming in to make their reports after bringing down two Me109s.

A Flying Officer pictured on his aircraft following a successful mission.

Acknowledgements

All photographs reproduced by the kind permission of the Trustees of the
Imperial War Museum, London.

The author would like to thank RAF Duxford, the Imperial War Museum
Sound, Film and Video, Photography and Document archives and
Tim Collier of the RAF for their generous assistance.

Also in the series:

CIVIL WAR
The Story of Thomas Adamson
England 1643-1650

TRAFALGAR
The Story of James Grant
HMS *Norseman* 1799-1806

The Story of Billy Stevens
The Western Front 1914-1918